OFFICIALLY NOTED

DIARY OF AN 8-BIT WARRIOR

CRAFTING ALLIANCES

This edition © 2017 by Andrews McMeel Publishing.

Published in French under the title *Journal d'un Noob (Méga Guerrier) Tome III*
© 2016 by 404 éditions, an imprint of Édi8, Paris, France
Text © 2015 by Cube Kid, Illustration © 2016 by Saboten

Andrews McMeel Publishing
a division of Andrews McMeel Universal
1130 Walnut Street, Kansas City, Missouri 64106
www.andrewsmcmeel.com

17 18 19 20 21 RR2 10 9 8 7 6 5 4 3 2 1

ISBN: 978-1-4494-8228-2

Library of Congress Control Number: 2016948376

Made by:
LSC Communications US, LLC
Address and location of manufacturer:
1009 Sloan Street
Crawfordsville, IN 47933
1st printing-12/09/16

• CUBE KID •

DIARY OF AN 8-BIT WARRIOR

CRAFTING ALLIANCES

Illustrations by
Saboten

Andrews McMeel Publishing®

a division of Andrews McMeel Universal

In memory of Lola Salines (1986–2015),
founder of 404 éditions and editor of this series,
who lost her life in the November 2015 attacks on Paris.
Thank you for believing in me.

– Cube Kid

MONDAY—EARLY MORNING

I woke up **before the sun even rose** and couldn't fall back asleep.

Of course, Mom and Dad didn't have this problem. They'd been working the fields all week.

Maybe that's why they **finally** warmed up to the idea of me becoming a warrior.

These days, **they're just too tired to argue.**

At least they decided to give me a **bigger** allowance.

I recalled the conversation with Mom the other day:

"Use these emeralds to enchant your robe with **Frost Protection II,** okay, **honey?** I don't want you getting sick!"

"I don't think there is such an enchantment, **but thanks anyway.**"

"**Okay, well, be sure to eat more steak!** Cookies won't keep your hunger bar up."

"But cookies are tasty . . ."

"And wear your leather armor underneath your robe today. If you fall again during training, **your health bar won't get so low.**"

1

"Mom. Armor doesn't protect against falling damage."

"Oh. All right, dear."

Jello was sound asleep as well. From inside his box, he made quiet little sounds—***burble, burble***—the baby slime equivalent of snoring. I put on my boots and grabbed **my sword** on my way out the door. It was still dark. But soon, as I made my way to school, **the square sun crawled** over the gloomy, gray houses and shed pink light upon the gloomy, gray streets. To a villager, this was a precious time. At this hour, the monsters were crawling back to a forest that never knew the sun. In their absence, a sleepy village was now **rustling awake.**

2

I went for **a morning jog.** I thought it'd help clear my mind. **It didn't.**

Five minutes in, my anger flared like a redstone torch . . . because I saw the posters. They're everywhere, **those posters.**

Pebble is on most of them . . .

I DON'T ALWAYS
KILL MOBS . . .

BUT WHEN I DO,
I KILL THEM
IN ONE SHOT.

3

There were nearly as many posters with Emerald, Steve, Mike, the mayor . . . and even Urf. Urf!

WANTED
GANKED OR AT MAX HEALTH

REWARD:
500 EMERALDS

He took off on Sunday, from what I heard, carrying half a village supply room with him. He took two donkeys, each with chests, that he loaded up before stuffing his own pockets—all three inventories filled with stacks of iron, enchanted books . . . in short, our most valuable items.

4

Definitely
turned traitor !!!
Definitely sided with the mobs.

And definitely offered them more than just piles of **shiny loot.** The right information can **be worth more** than diamonds, and that would explain how the **mobs pinpointed our school so easily.** He left a trail of items on his way out of town. **The heaviest stuff.** Weapons. Armor. He was most likely weighed down. He most likely wanted to escape quickly.

Fear is stronger than greed.

A few posters had **the names of many who fought** on Saturday. The posters didn't have any pictures, but I'm including them in this diary. They fought **just as hard as** Pebble did, after all . . .

Hold on, Weston!!!

WESTON	CHARLIE	GABE
HEATHER	BOSTON	CAMERON
MIA	BECK	RAFI
MARY	GRYFFEN	SAM
EMMA	CASA	BLOOTY
SOPHIA	DYLAN	JAKEY
BRIGID	KHAN	ZAK
LUNA	GABE	NOAH
ALYSSA	DAN	OWEN
ANDREA	MICRO	RHETT
MARISA	MATTHEW	JOEY
RACHEL V	THOMAS	JAMIN
AILEEN	ANTHONY	SIMONE
JOAN	THOM	JOSH
GRACE	SPARROW	CLARK
ZAYNE	PAUL	KYLE
MERIEDI	BRAD	HAYDEN
TOMOYA	LINCOLN	JAY
WILL	ANDREW	OSCAR
BRENNAN	ALEX	SAMUEL
MARCO	JAMES	REMY
TOBI	FINN	JACK
WESTON	ELLIS	CADYN
SCOOEY	FRANKIE	RYAN

Hello, Gabe.

Good luck, Ryan!

6

Suddenly, **a freezing wind picked up.** I raised the collar on my robe. Then I glanced at the distant houses, wondering whether Breeze **could be out there, somewhere,** at this early hour . . .

Who *is she?*

Was she telling the truth?

Did her father really send

her to spy on me?

When it comes to her, there's **only one thing I know for sure** . . . I glanced down at **my health bar,** at the row of little red hearts, **and remembered** . . .

I entered the school and walked empty halls. I checked every empty classroom. Surprisingly, one room was occupied. **The head teacher's office on the second floor.** *Professor* . . . Brio?

7

He smirked. "Morning."

I nodded. "Morning."

By the way, we weren't **exchanging greetings**—we were stating a welcome fact. I sat down, either *on some stairs* or *in a chair*, depending on which universe you come from.

"I take it you're **the head teacher** now," I said.

"**Something like that.**" He adjusted his glasses—I caught a glimpse of his purple eyes. "I'll be overseeing everyone's progress from here on out. I suppose you could say it's time **to kick things up a . . . notch.**"

He rose. "Come with me."

8

I followed him to the tower—**to the very top**—where we looked out at **the eastern wall.**

"I must say," Brio murmured, "I'm **surprised** they were able to **rebuild** that mushroom shop as well as they did." He turned to me. "I believe you caused more damage there than a wither blast."

"Sorry. I just didn't . . ."

9

"You survived. You used what you had and survived. Honestly, I'm impressed. Of course, you couldn't have done that without Breeze's help. She saved you. Surely you're wondering how she managed that."

"Yes. How?"

"Leaping IV, Swiftness II, Strength III, Stoneskin V. That last one costs a fortune to craft . . . and has a very bad taste from what I understand."

I blinked. "Potions?"

"Yes. She chugged so many she made herself sick. That's why she's staying home today. Her father insists."

"So, that's it, huh? . . . Potions."

"You were expecting a more interesting explanation. Special powers. Magic, perhaps."

"I guess so."

"Cheer up, then. True magic does exist, beyond enchantments and potion effects . . . and someday, we will reclaim it."

Reclaim . . . ? As in, get back? As in, we once had magic?! I couldn't believe what I was hearing. Before I could ask,

10

however, Brio continued: "By the way, I understand the pigman had a weapon that found its way into your inventory. I will take that from you now."

"What? Why?"

"You really need to ask?"

"Whatever." I handed him Urkk's hook. "I was never that into fishing, anyway. Besides, knowing my luck, if I tried using that thing, I'd reel in a creeper by accident."

Brio smirked again, stuffed the weapon into a pocket, and turned back to the streets below.

"Beautiful, isn't it? This is the last remaining village in all of eastern Minecraftia. For hundreds of thousands of blocks in every direction, nothing else remains."

"Nothing?"

He shook his head. "There are survivors, I've heard, scattered here and there. But they're all hiding underground now. We are, perhaps, Minecraftia's only hope."

". . ."

11

"As the mobs **evolve,** so too must our village. We will **fortify our walls. Upgrade our defenses. Create new weapons.** Research more efficient farming methods. Push ourselves to the very limit. This is Minecraftia's last stand against Herobrine."

". . ."

He turned to me. **"It's going to be quite a show."**

MONDAY—LATER

Well, Brio wasn't joking. Those strange men in black robes really did kick things up a notch. They were everywhere at school. They also carried sticks. No. Not carried. Wielded. And threateningly so.

This one kid, Rock—he's not a bad student: decent scores, knows how to use a sword. But he was hanging around in the hall for too long after Mob History II started, chatting with his friends. Well, one of those guys came up to him and tapped him on the shoulder with a stick. "What's wrong with you, punk?" stick guy barked. "The mobs don't goof off and skip class. The only thing they skip is lunch, so they can study even more!"

"B-but . . . I'm n-not a m-mob—"

"I'll say! The mobs probably don't talk back to their superiors!" He jabbed Rock with his stick. "This is your second offense! Don't make a third!"

We heard it all from inside the classroom. We soon found out what happens during a third offense.

After Rock sat down, he started looking around, looking out the window, anywhere but at the teacher. Minutes later, two of those

13

guys burst into the room, charged up, and pulled Rock out of his chair so fast they literally yanked him **out of his boots.**

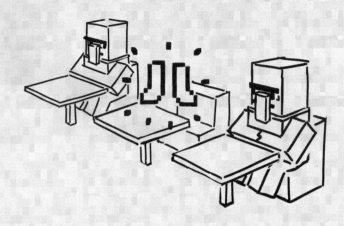

Suddenly, the teacher's **lecture on mob history** became
the most interesting thing
in the universe.

After seeing that, **we took notes.** We paid **attention.** We stared forward and **nodded our heads enthusiastically.** Anything to **prevent a visit from them,** who could be lurking anywhere out there in the hall.

Mr. Beetroot, the history teacher, continued: "After several months of existing in the **Overworld,** a zombie will **turn into** a skeleton. The skeleton will grow **smarter.** The skeleton will run away if injured."

14

Meanwhile, I thought: *After* **thirty minutes** *of* **Mob History II,** *Runt will turn into a* **zombie.** *Runt will make* **moaning sounds.** *Runt will head toward the nearest door and break it down.*

Even Pebble **wasn't immune to their harassment anymore.** After Mob History, he was chatting with **Sara** in the hall. Their backs were to Pebble's locker.

Brio, like a creeper who'd chugged **an invisibility potion,** crept up to the locker and looted it while the two of them talked.

Pebble whirled around. "**Hey!** That's my *stuff,* **endernoob!**"

Brio smiled. "If by '**hey**' you mean '**sir**,' by '**my**' you mean '**your**,' and by '**endernoob**' you mean '**I really hope you enjoy those delicious steaks because you're awesome and amazing**,' then yes, you are absolutely correct."

"Um . . . **what?**"

"**First offense.** Don't be late again."

Of course, come lunchtime, the first thing Pebble did was head to the cafeteria. **Guess** who was serving?

15

I'm joking.

If *he* was serving, the food might have actually been interesting.

Steak wouldn't have been on the menu, but anything a cow might have offered would have been infinitely better than what was available today.

You see, some of Brio's men were behind the counter, and they'd cooked up something **extra special** for all the kids on the "naughty students who must be punished" list.

You want some **mud soup?**

"No? Okay, then. How about some coarse dirt stew?
A gravel sandwich? Cooked spider legs? Still no?
Then why not skip to dessert?
You can try a slice of our nice slime pie."

Look, I get it. I understand what they're doing. They're toughening us up for when the real battles begin. They're forcing us to pay attention. To remember everything. To never make mistakes. Someday, our lives will depend on it. I know that.

But isn't this going a little too far?

The average age of a student is twelve, after all. Sure, we're no longer a single block tall and golems no longer hand us poppies when they're bored . . . but we're still kids.

Aren't we?

It didn't get any easier for Pebble. During the daily running drill, they were screaming at him constantly. I will say, even though he's a punk, he didn't lose his cool. Even when Drill and two others were shouting at him at the same time. It seemed like his mind was elsewhere.

17

The whole time we ran, Brio **walked among us,** arms crossed. His voice was raised in a **dull monotone:** "The mobs have retreated once again . . .

"But they *will* return, and **who knows what they'll try next?**

"Becoming a **good warrior** is why you pay attention in class . . .

"Defending your village is why you spend hours reading about mobs.

"You swing swords at **practice dummies** so future generations can live in peace.

"Someday, we'll all live on **a sandy beach . . .**

"We'll eat cocoa beans.

"We'll drink watermelon juice.

18

"We'll work on our tans, which is something zombies can never do. Perhaps that's why they **dislike us so much.**"

I have a dream . . .

You'll **love** to do your homework.

19

You'll *listen* to your teachers.

You will train at least **five hours** per day, you **bedrock-digging** . . .

Pufferfish-eating . . .

Enderman-*chasing* . . .

20

Gold armor-
wearing . . .

Cactus
jockeys!!!

At first glance, one might think that this is perhaps **a new type of slime mob.**

Nah. **It's just me,** um . . . resting.

Yeah. **Resting.**

(Hey, at least I didn't collapse facedown in some dirt.)

21

It's getting even **more competitive** at school too. In those brief moments when students could actually hang out between classes, everyone stood around in their **little groups.**

- Team Craft;
- Team Noob;
- Team All Girls;
- Team Redstone;
- Team Pebble *(growing in number);*
- Team Emerald *(good friends with Team Pebble).*

And, of course, **Team Runt,** which everyone seems to be against lately.

Why? What happened to kids asking me for building advice? What happened to the **"green egg kid"?** No one had even **congratulated** me on Saturday. I took down a big boss using a bigger mushroom, and there was almost **no mention of it.**

In fact, I was walking down the hall with my friends today, and **Ariel** gave us what I call **"the look."**

22

First, she glared at us. Tilted her head. Rolled her eyes. Moved her shoulders in a confrontational way. Then, she turned back to Emerald and Sara, said something, and glared at us again while Sara did the same. Whatever they were saying, it wasn't good.

Other times, as I passed different groups of kids, I heard stuff like:

"What's his level now?"

"I'm way better at farming than her."

"She actually calls herself a warrior?"

"Hey, have you seen her record book?"

"He's still wearing those hideous brown robes."

"I totally saw Pebble and Sara *hanging out the other day* . . ."

"I heard Runt and **that weird girl** . . . what's her name again? *Anyway*, Ariel said they took out **a giant pigman**. Not that *I* believe it. **Those two noobs? Pssh. Come on.**"

Before it was time for class, the **"teams"** strolled down the hall together, real **slow**. At one point, **Team Pebble** passed **Team Redstone**. They gave each other **"the look,"** did the whole shoulder thing, the head tilting, and took off to their respective classes.

I'm better than him.

We're better than them.

That girl's trash-tier.

That kid's an übernoob.

What kind of armor do they have?

Even the members of **Team Noob** look down on me now. Including that kid with the **combat score of a door.**

**Welcome
to my life.**

24

It's always been like this, ever since school started—but lately, things have **gotten way worse.**

I wonder if it's the same way **on Earth?**

Later today, there was a **special after-school activity: digging a deadfall field.**

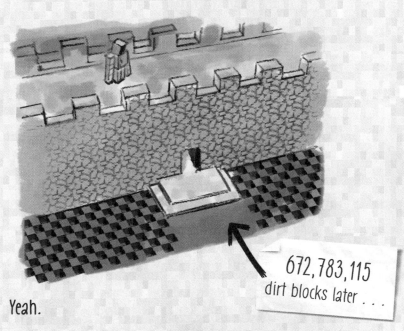

672,783,115 dirt blocks later . . .

Yeah.

After digging about **two hundred holes** myself, it feels as though I've dunked my hands in **lava.** Oh, and don't ask what that golem is doing up there on the wall.

25

No one knows.
It's kind of a mystery.

The only way to get up onto the wall is by climbing a ladder, and the last time I checked, golems couldn't do that. Who knows—maybe the golems are getting smarter, too. Just like the mobs. Maybe next year a golem will be running for mayor.

I'd vote for him.

Speaking of the mayor, he gave a speech just before dinnertime.

"We will build our walls so high and so thick," he shouted, "any travelers mapping this area will think they've run into an Extreme Hills Biome!!"

Everyone cheered at this.

"Let the mobs attack!! Let the creepers blow themselves up all night! In the morning, we'll come out and thank them for helping us mine dirt and sand!! We'll thank them since we won't have to wear down our shovels!!"

More cheers—
it was ten times louder than Drill's shouting.

"The eastern wall . . . will not fall!!!"

Remember everything that happened in school yesterday? Today was exactly the same.

Shoot better!

I've seen birch doors hit harder!!!

If you do not do your homework, it will be your turn.

28

Also, there *was* a new, um, special activity today: Escaping Zombies I. Drill changed into a dark green robe and painted his face with lime-green dye. He was the zombie. He also hid in the weirdest places.

Imagine this: One second you're just going to your next class, on time, minding your own business. And you think: *I listened in my last class. I wrote things down. I asked some questions. Things are going good.*

Then someone looking very much like a freaky cross between a zombie, a witch, and a creeper bursts out of a supply room nearby. Roaring. Slobbering. Running straight for you.

GRAAAAAAAAAAAAA

AAAARGRGRGRG!!!

Slobber—running down his chin—mixed with green dye to resemble watery slime. Cave spiders, please move over. This is real terror.

I'm not sure whether the green drool was intentional or what, but if Drill's goal was to make the girls scream louder than a note block on the highest setting . . .

well, mission accomplished.

(the boys screamed too . . .)

I mean, no one had told us about this. Everyone thought he was a new kind of zombie. As one might expect, anyone Drill caught was humiliated: They had to wear a dark green robe like his for the rest of the day. By the way, that was just the start for those poor kids.

Later, Pebble, Donkey, and Rock took out their anger on such kids by dunking them in a well.

I wasn't one of them, though.

Not today. No, my friends!

When Drill burst through that door, I ran so fast I could've passed for an enderman, had I been wearing purple sunglasses and a black or dark gray robe.

30

By the way, for the past **three days,** we've had to help repair some damaged areas of the village. That didn't **work out so well.** I mean, *my* building score is pretty good, but . . . let's just say there are some kids who can't say the same. **They made many, many mistakes**—otherwise known as . . . Building Fails. *(For any of my dear readers on Earth, I will point out that building in this world isn't as easy as building in the computer game. Ever tried lugging a block of cobblestone around? Try it sometime.)*

BUILDING FAIL #1

Maybe this is some kind of modern art?

BUILDING FAIL #2

Honestly, who needs stairs? Falling is way faster.

BUILDING FAIL #3

Well, it's only a three-block jump to get to the second floor. It's to keep us in shape, see?

BUILDING FAIL #4

The buttonless iron door. Without a button to press, mobs will never be able to open it! Brilliant!! Oh, wait . . .

BUILDING FAIL #5

This button is reserved for endermen.

33

BUILDING FAIL #6

Window? Door? What's the difference?

BUILDING FAIL #7

Needless to say, this Building Fail didn't stick around for long. Same goes for the building itself. I guess no one told him that wood and lava do not get along well.

34

BUILDING FAIL #8

Because opening a wooden door the normal way—you know, with your hand—just isn't cool anymore.

BUILDING FAIL #9

To enter this garden, you have to do a backflip over a fence; obviously, a ninja/farmer built this.

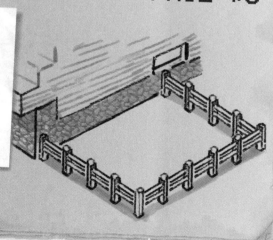

BUILDING FAIL #10

Apparently, an enderman built this house. He doesn't need a door. He just teleports inside.

BUILDING FAIL #11

Ummm, this has to be someone's attempt at trolling. I mean, we've got some real noobs in my village, but no one is this bad . . .

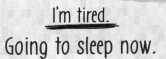

I'm tired.
Going to sleep now.

36

WEDNESDAY

Did you sleep well? No? Too bad!

Run faster.

Work more.

"There was once a man named **Herobrine**," Brio called out as we **ran** and **ran.** "Sorry. Not once. He's still alive. *Anyway* . . .

"He's lived for a **very long time** . . .

"He's seen this **world's earliest days** . . .

37

"He lived at a time when there were **towns, castles,** and **vast kingdoms** instead of just **simple villages** . . .

"When **ancient temples** weren't ancient . . .

"When desert temples weren't buried in sand . . .

"When abandoned mine shafts weren't abandoned . . .

"When villagers weren't known as villagers, but another name, long since forgotten . . .

HEROBRINE
IS COMING FOR YOU.

AND YOU,
AND YOU, YEAH, YOU TOO.
OH, AND THAT COW OVER
THERE. (PLUS THAT GUY
HIDING IN THE TREE.)

"When there was such a thing as magic.

"This is what we are up against.

"This is the enemy we face.

"We must not let him win."

Just like on Monday, I was so exhausted after training that, again, I collapsed face-first in some grass.

At least nothing bad has happened to me lately, I thought.

I haven't been yelled at too much.

I haven't been singled out.

It's not so bad.

But when I rolled onto my back and opened my eyes . . .

Drill was staring down at me.

39

"Congratulations, Runt. Your unit has been selected for a special role in **Project Squidboat**."

I rubbed my eyes. "That's, um . . . **great**, sir, but . . . what's Project Squidboat?"

The combat teacher gave me **a toothy grin**. I'm just thankful he wasn't shouting, since his face was a block from mine.

"**Tomorrow**, you and Emerald are **going outside the wall**."

I didn't say anything, but I thought:

*Oh, okay. **That's all, then.***
*We'll just go outside and **wave to the mobs.***
*Maybe go into their **cozy little forest***
*and join them for some **tea and cookies.***

40

So, today . . . Project Squidboat has officially started. Basically, it's a class on, um . . . "mob psychology." In other words, the mayor wants to learn more about how the mobs think. For whatever reason, my combat unit was chosen to do the dirty work. Since Breeze *still* isn't at school, and since Urf isn't around anymore, that meant . . . it was just Emerald and me.

Hurrr.

Okay, let's go over what Project Squidboat is all about.

See that pile of cobblestone over there? That was an area Brio called "the building site," or simply "the site." Emerald

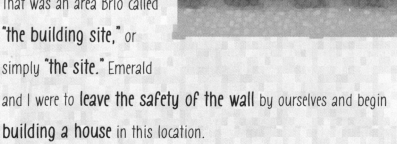

and I were to leave the safety of the wall by ourselves and begin building a house in this location.

41

At the same time, the rest of the students were to stand on the wall with **bows and arrows** while they watched us build.

What was **the purpose** of this, you ask?

The idea was we'd build a house in front of the mobs' forest . . . and **see what the mobs did.** Would they **attack** the house? Would they totally destroy it? My guess was that the mobs weren't going to dance around, hold hands, and **sing songs.**

But apparently **Brio** and **Drill** needed us to build a house in order to figure that out. Of course, one might ask *why* grown adults sent **two twelve-year-olds** outside instead of going out themselves.

Real brave, those guys.

"First," said Brio, "we want you two to make an **odd-looking** house."

"The **weirdest** house you can possibly imagine," Drill added.

"**Of course!**" Emerald flashed them a grin. "Leave it to us! Our house will be the strangest house you've ever seen! **Funky** with a **capital** *F* !"

With these words, she patted me on the back and gave me a look that said: *Don't say anything to make them angry, noob, because I don't feel like doing one hundred push-ups right now.*

Then she pushed me forward and said, "I think it's time for someone *strong and brave* to lead this project."

Great.

I took a deep breath,
staring at the gate in front of us.

The gate in the eastern wall is a dual-lever-operated iron door system. If one door is blown up, there's still another door to keep the mobs at bay—another village "building code."

Fun fact: The doors can be opened only from the inside. Another fact: When Emerald and I stepped out into the plains, Drill shut the gate behind us. And yet another fact: When Drill shut the gate, I wanted to cry. And dig a hole in the ground. And cover the hole with dirt. And curl up into a ball.

Emerald was looking all around. "Listen," she said, "you build the house and I'll uh . . . I'll watch your back."

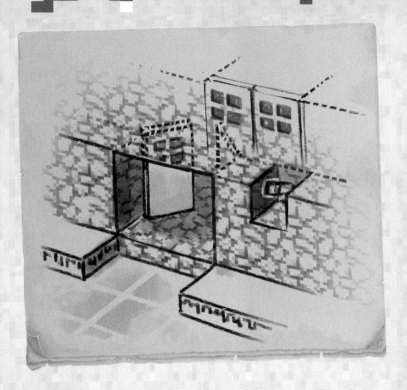

"Why me?"

"C'mon. Screamy wants us to build a weird-looking house, right? That's your thing."

"What's *that* supposed to mean?"

She rolled her eyes. "Dude, you made a furnace house. You defeated a boss with a giant mushroom. You're pretty much the king of weird. Besides, you have absolutely *no* fashion sense. I mean, look at your robe! And that cloak!"

44

"Whatever." I grabbed a block of sand from my inventory. "As long as it means you'll stop talking."

She crossed her arms and looked away. "Y'know, you can be such a jerk!"

But she looked back when I started digging and placing the foundation-sand.

"What are you doing?!" she hissed. "We're supposed to build a house, not a sand castle."

I ignored her, keeping my eye on the forest . . . just in case the mobs decided to rush us. The slightest movement out there and I was gone. If a cloud looked too strange, or if some bat gave me a funny look—poof—even a mine cart on powered rails would have nothing on me. NOTHING. I didn't see anything moving around, though. Soon, my masterpiece was finished.

"As I said, you're weird!!!"

Yeah. A cactus house.
With a roof made of melon blocks.

Drill had given us a ton of **building materials,** after all. It was pretty much the **strangest building** I could think of, given the supplies. When we got back, Drill wasn't just smiling—he was beaming like an enderman in a desert . . . he was beaming like a creeper in a cat-free zone . . . like a **mooshroom named Binky.** That last one probably doesn't make sense to you.

46

You see, **Binky** was this mooshroom I met once, and it was, like, **ten times happier** than a normal cow.

So, like . . . smiling like that mooshroom means . . . smiling a lot.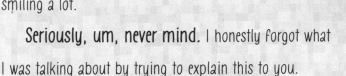

Seriously, um, never mind. I honestly forgot what I was talking about by trying to explain this to you.

Anyway, **Drill was happy,** okay?

"**Well done,**" he said. "Well done . . . **like a noob hugging a blaze!**"

(Wow, that analogy was even worse than my mooshroom one! I feel a lot better now.)

Still looking at my house, Brio **nodded** in approval. Then I took a spot on the wall with **Max** and **Stump,** who **applauded** my new creation. But **Pebble, Donkey,** and **Rock** said it was the **stupidest-looking** house they'd ever seen.

Um, wasn't that the point . . . ?
Noobs!

47

Then, we **waited,** hidden behind the raised sections of wall.

Before long, a **group of zombies** rushed out of the forest to inspect my **cactus house.** They were speaking in the **ancient tongue** again, so I couldn't understand what they were saying . . . but they were obviously **confused.**

urgaburgauuuguu???
buururrrrguurgurg
gurbu.

Then the zombies **got angry.** They took out some **axes** and began **chopping at my cactus house.** They chopped and chopped until there was almost nothing left except for a few **cactus blocks scattered**

in the sand. They actually took most of it with them. One zombie even roared angrily, and then he kicked a mined cactus block as hard as he could. It went sailing off into the plains.

My lovely cactus house!
How could they be so disrespectful?!

After the zombies vanished into the woods, Drill stood up.

"So the greenies aren't as bright as we thought," he said. "Runt's house confused them for a second, anyway."

Emerald sighed. "That doesn't mean much. Runt's house had *me* confused."

"It's not very hard to confuse you," Max said.

"Hmmph!"

"Now, don't fight," said Brio. "Because you two are going back out there."

Emerald and I looked at each other before exclaiming simultaneously:

"What?!"

It was **Stage II of Project Squidboat.** This time, we had to build **a beautiful house.** Princess Whinerella decided to be the one to build that. Her house was what one might expect . . . **except she** added a sign. **I forgot to do that.**

> I think they will **appreciate** the icing on the cake.

> ZOMBIES STINK. TO DEATH.

Again, **we took off back to the wall.** And again, the zombies came to **inspect** the house. A zombie took one look at the sign, **grunted** angrily, and kicked the sign over. Then the zombie shouted something, and **even more zombies came out.**

"They don't seem to **notice us**," Max whispered.

He was right. We were hiding, but there were over **a hundred** of us. Surely *one* of them should have seen us **peeking** from behind the wall.

"They must have **really poor eyesight**," I whispered back. "Maybe it's the sunlight."

Stump nodded. "We could use this to our advantage somehow."

Hmm. Maybe **Project Squidboat** wasn't such a bad idea. We've **learned a lot** about the mobs today.

By this time, the zombies were **chattering away** in their **low, guttural** language. Then they totally **trashed Emerald's cute little house.** One zombie stomped on every flower. Another zombie even tried **eating a flower.**

By the way, the zombie was eating a blue orchid, which was roughly the same color as his shirt. So in this picture, it kinda looks like he's eating his own shirt. He wasn't, though. Of course, I could have changed the flower to, say, a pink tulip or something. But I'm going for accuracy here.

51

As if that **wasn't enough,** a creeper rushed in and exploded.

There was nothing left.

Drill came over to us when the mobs went back into the trees. "Well, **that's it** for today," he said. "I think we've made some real progress today in **understanding** the enemy."

I stood up.

"Wait, sir. I . . . I'd like **to try something else.** I wanna go back out there."

A few students gasped. **Even Brio looked shocked.**

"What is it, Runt?"

"It's hard to explain." I paused. "**Um,** can **I . . . um . . . err . . . have a stack of obsidian?"**

At the mention of **obsidian,** Drill got angry. "**OBSIDIAN?! WHAT ARE YOU—**"

I was already **preparing** myself to do **two hundred push-ups.** Maybe **three hundred.** *(Note: Someday, if I ever become a combat teacher, there will be no push-ups—only pumpkin pie-eating contests.)*

Brio interrupted him. He grabbed Drill and walked down the wall some ways away, and the two of them talked for a **long time.** Drill was making all sorts of gestures—obviously, he thought obsidian would be **wasted** on a project like this.

When they finally came back, Brio said, "We have only **one stack of obsidian** left in the village supply. Urf took the other stack. **Will you make good use of it?**"

I nodded. "I'm sure."

"You're really sure?"

"Really sure."

"You're **really, really, really sure?** You will use this obsidian **wisely?**"

"**Really, really, really** sure with an **endercreeper** on top. I will wisely use this obsidian."

"Okay then. **Here's your obsidian.**"

(It didn't go exactly like that. But I'm just trying to stress how worried they were.)

Here's how worried they were: Brio and Drill worriedly exchanged worried glances of worryfulness. **Enchanted with Worryfulness VII.**

53

(Worryfulness is probably not an Earth word. If there's something like the **Intergalactic Committee on Proper Spelling,** please don't report me to them. If you don't report me, and you visit me in my village someday, I will have Stump personally bake you either three cookies or one cake. Your choice.)

All right, so Brio gave me **a stack of obsidian.**

By the way, I need to thank the **builder noobs** for this idea—the kids behind all those building mistakes. Within a minute, I was back outside, working on **house number three.** I know I've been talking about mooshrooms and worryfulness and having my best friend bake you stuff.

I'm only twelve, okay?!
My mind **wanders.**

The important thing here is that I was *building a house made of obsidian.*

Yes. An obsidian house was being built.

Actually, it wasn't so much a house as it was a . . . **uh** . . . **well,** I don't really know *what* you'd call it.

THE CUBE.
What does it do?

A simple five-by-five box. A large cube made entirely of obsidian. It had no doors, no windows, and no mechanisms of any kind. It could withstand creeper blasts, TNT blasts, and any tool less than diamond. Remember Boom Mountain? The mountain made entirely of TNT? This cube could withstand that. All of that.

That's how awesome a cube made of obsidian is. Not only was it mysterious, but the mobs had no way of destroying it. Unless they had diamond pickaxes. (And let's face it, if the mobs have diamond pickaxes, well, we've already lost this war—wasting a stack of obsidian wouldn't matter.)

55

The zombies came back a third time, thoroughly confused. They punched the cube. (Why?!) Kicked it. Swung stone pickaxes at it. Three creepers even blew up right next to it. And when the smoke cleared, the cube was still there, unharmed, silently mocking their attempts. After that, the zombies dropped their pickaxes and ran back into the woods.

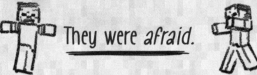

They were afraid.

"Interesting," Max said. "Fear of the unknown is the strongest type of fear. I read that somewhere."

Stump patted me on the back. "Good work, dude. They'll spend days trying to figure that thing out. That means we can relax. I really need to get some baking done!!"

Drill didn't know what to make of the cube. He was standing on the edge of the wall, studying it, scratching his chin and muttering to himself. When I turned to Brio . . . he was studying me. In silence. Was he angry? Did I do something wrong . . . ?

Maybe I had wasted the only
obsidian our village had. For nothing . . .

56

FRIDAY

Yeah, there was **a lot more training** today. But forget the training.

Dude, complaining about training is so two days ago.

By Friday afternoon, **everyone was talking about the cube.** After school got out, practically everyone in the village was up on the wall, **watching.**

"All we need is **popcorn**," Mike said to Steve.

Steve got the same look he gets when he's talking about **pizza.**

"Oh, man. Butter? **Caramel?** I'd pay fifty emeralds for even *plain* popcorn! **What am I saying?!** I'd eat popcorn kernels *raw* without even **cooking** them! Actually, what am I watching this cube for?! I should be working on recipes!"

Mike facepalmed. "Why did I mention popcorn? **Why?**"

"**Will you two noobs be quiet?!**" Pebble hissed. "You're gonna **scare off** the mobs!"

Yeah, those mobs sure were **hard at work.** It was interesting watching them **struggle with** that huge obsidian block. You see, the mobs just couldn't stand it. They just *had* to find out what was up with that thing. They wouldn't be able to rest until they **blew it all up**—or destroyed **just a single block** so they could find out what was inside. *(There was nothing inside. Tee-hee. Just a torch.)*

They built **a dirt staircase** alongside it . . .

Then creepers climbed the staircase. **Oh, yeah,** that iron golem was still hanging around.

He looked really sad, too, with his head always lowered like that. Anyway, back to the cube—

— Also, bring your own armor enchanted with Blast Protection V.

CREEPER PARTY
FLINT AND STEEL
NOT SUPPLIED

59

The zombie down below started shouting:

"Urgbo! Jorgbo! **Gurggo!**"

Emerald: "Uhhh, I'm assuming he was counting to three. Anyone else come to that conclusion?"

I guess the zombie was trying to **make sure** the creepers exploded at **exactly the same time.** Not that it helped. According to Max, it just **didn't matter.**

60

WELL, ON P. 81 OF *THE PUDDLES BUILDING HANDBOOK,* IT SAYS, "NO AMOUNT OF EXPLOSIVES CAN DAMAGE OBSIDIAN."

MAX—THE WALKING WIKIPEDIA.

Anyway, the mobs tried a lot of stuff.

TNT. Lots of TNT.

Charged creepers.

Enchanted iron pickaxes.

Blocks of TNT mixed with charged creepers.

They even tried digging under it to see whether there was an obsidian floor.

Pssh. Just LOL @ them.

As if *I* wouldn't have thought of that! My building score is 97 now, the nooblords. The zombies spent like fifteen minutes digging under that thing. And the whole time they were probably thinking, **Ohhhhh, we're gonna dig under it! Ohhhh, we're clever!** Then they discovered—oh, so there *is* an obsidian floor.

LOL

One zombie, after he came back up to the surface, was **so angry** that he kept beating the ground with his shovel, **over** and **over.**

"Dude, that zombie looks really, **really mad.**"

Eventually, it started pouring, and the mobs **called it a day.**

Stump sighed. "Rained away."

"**Show's over,** folks," the mayor called out. "It'll be dark soon. Everyone please go inside."

I said good-bye to Stump and Max. Emerald was looking at me while I did.

It seemed **she wanted to say something to me,** although I couldn't imagine what. I walked past her and took off back home through the wet streets . . .

thinking about Breeze,

and what she might be doing . . .

SATURDAY—MORNING

Well, the mobs didn't attack the cube much today. From what I heard, every hour or so a new zombie had walked up and swung a pickaxe at it, then retreated back into the forest. He probably heard about the cube from the other zombies and wanted to take the "obsidian cube challenge." You're probably not a cool zombie unless you do that.

In other news . . . I'm seriously freaking out about Breeze. What happened to her? Where did she go? She didn't show up to school the whole week, and I have no idea where she lives. And since I'm apparently her only friend, there's no real way to find out. I'm about to go door to door until I find her.

Be back later, Diary.

UPDATE:

I didn't find Breeze. As luck would have it, the third door I knocked on swung open . . . to reveal Emerald. And here's the thing: She wanted to talk. She insisted.

63

"I've been, um, wanting to get **something off my chest,**" she said. "I realized you're not such **a bad guy.** What you did yesterday was **pretty cool,** actually. So with that being said, I kinda wanna **apologize** for running away last Saturday. I mean, that pigman was **crazy huge,** you know?"

I eyed her cool-looking cloak. "**Happens to the best of us.**"

At this, the so-called war **heroine** poked me in the chest. "Hey! I *did* manage to get some **iron golems!** I'm not a wuss, **okay?!**"

"Sure. You're not a wuss."

Anger **flashed across her face.** She **poked** me again. "You might think you're **hot stuff,** but honestly, your social skills need **a lot of work!** All you do is rage, show off, and **act like a total tryhard!**"

Tryhard? Really . . . ?

Emerald narrowed her eyes. "I don't suppose you heard what my friends **said about you** in the hall the other day?"

"No, and **I don't particularly care.**"

"You should. You're well on your way to becoming **the least popular** boy in school." Suddenly, her anger vanished, and **she smiled.**

64

"So you should consider yourself lucky, because I'm willing to help you out. Let me teach you how to be cool and likable. I mean, with the way Pebble's been treating you, you really need more friends."

I peered at her suspiciously. "And what would *you* be getting in return?"

"I wanna join your team."

"Um, you *are* on my team. And what a team it is. Between you and Urf, the mobs pretty much have no chance. You know the giant pigman? He didn't explode from TNT. He was just thinking *Oh, man, Emerald and Urf are coming for me; I really don't want to have to deal with this*, and then he swallowed a charged creeper."

"Not funny. Anyway, I'm not talking about that, silly. I wanna join Team Runt. I want to roll with you guys. You, that baker kid, the bookworm, and . . . Breeze."

Wait. Wait, wait, wait. So Emerald was saying . . . she actually wants to be a part of *Team Runt?* Ms. Popularity actually wants to hang out with a kid who's been dunked in water more times than a farmer's bucket?

65

"It's funny, when you think about it," she said. "They're teaching us all this stuff in school, like advanced crafting, redstone circuits . . . but they never teach us anything about how to make a friend."

Her words slowly sank in. Friends are important. I had learned that with Stump.

But equally important is not having too many enemies.

Friends matter! Without Breeze, I'd probably be in Urkk's inventory as an item called "Villager Stew." If I knew how to make more friends, Pebble and his crew wouldn't be able to harass me so much! Life is other people, isn't it?! If there was no one else in this village . . . if it was just me and a bunch of blocks . . . how boring would that life be? The thing that matters most is the people around me.

I go to the bakery to buy cookies so I can eat. I'm trying to become a warrior so I can protect my family. Every day I pray that Pebble and Donkey don't do something horrible to me. And all those things involve . . . speaking to other people. Making friends. Not making enemies. Being "likable," as she puts it. Emerald really has something there.

66

Why don't they teach us anything about this in school?!

And, honestly, I was such a **jerk** to Breeze. At first, **I totally ignored her!** And, yeah, a lot of kids *did* ask for my help—but I'd ignored them too! No wonder kids at school glare at me in the halls lately . . .

I nodded. Stood up **straighter.**

"**Okay,**" I said. "Let's say I agree with **you.** What then? **Where do we start?**"

Emerald's face **lit up** like a **sea lantern.**

"I know just the thing. **Follow me.**"

SATURDAY—AFTERNOON

SALES

LATEST STYLES

AUTHENTIC WOOL

Yeah. Emerald took me to the **biggest clothing shop** in the village. **The Clothing Castle.** It's owned by Puddles. Apparently, he's not only **a master builder** but a **fashion designer** as well. As you can see, it's a **huge** place. A bunch of girls from school work as **assistants** here: **Heather, Mia, Mary, Emma.** They love **crafting clothes.**

68

Oh, and Sophia and her brother, Ryan. *(Ryan's into combat like I am, so he helps Puddles come up with new types of leather armor.)* Puddles had recently hired Tomoya, a kid from school, as a new assistant. Is this information boring you? Stump said I should include more details about our village, so . . .

Anyway, Emerald said the first step in getting more people to like me is . . . buying a new robe. I glanced down at myself.

"Is there something wrong with this one?"

She sighed. "Look, I'm not saying you need to buy some diamond-encrusted outfits or something, but dude . . . if you want people to respect you, you have to stop walking around in that ratty old thing."

I am not wearing that.

"Ratty? Come on! It barely even has any mold spots!"

"Urggh. You're seriously hopeless."

Apparently it isn't okay to have mold spots on your robe. Who knew? I gave in and looked around at the various garments. Most of the robes were like this.

69

Emerald held up another robe in front of me. "Why don't you try this one on?"

"It's bright pink. Want us to match, do ya?"

"How about bright green?"

"No."

"Bright purple, then?"

"No."

"Fine, what about baby blue?"

I gave her a look that said: no

(That's a "no" without a period. You see, not including a period means you simply don't want to take the time to end the sentence completely. It means you care so little about what was just asked that you can't be bothered with taking the fraction of a second out of your day to add the period in.)

And finally . . . . Emerald picked out the worst robe in the whole store.

Yellowish-greenish brown.

"This isn't so bad, huh?"

". . . It's the color of baby poo."

70

"Sigh. You're so frustrating to shop with."

Then Puddles himself came over. He must have overheard us.

"Ahh, vat a strong young mahn! A fucha warrior, I see! I hev just zi sing for you!" He turned around. "Tomoya! Where's zat special suit? Zi dark gray one?"

Tomoya came over and guided us to whatever robe Puddles was talking about. It was slightly hidden in a corner.

WoW !
WoWOwOWO
WOwoWOw !

It was the coolest outfit I'd ever seen.

71

It even came with some kind of **hood and a special pair of boots** . . . In a robe like that, even *mobs* would **respect you.** If they didn't **break down crying** and beg you not to **crit them.**

Emerald, however, **groaned.** "You **can't go to school** in something like that. Especially not while wearing **the hood.** It's a little **creepy.** You'll become the **boy version of Breeze.**"

Whatever. I bought it **immediately.**

I bought a **second one** for Stump. *(Emerald suggested that.)*

Then I asked Emerald to draw me afterward.

CHECK OUT MY NEW GEAR, YO.

Looks pretty cool, right? If you don't think so, it's just Emerald's drawing ability. I asked her not to make it look as cool as it does in real life. Because you'd probably come to this world, head to my village, and steal it from me. By the way, the hood can be removed at any time. That's great, because we can't wear hats in school, and the same thing probably goes for ninja masks . . . (Sigh.)

"By the way," Emerald said, "you can dye that just like you can with leather armor. How about blue?"

"Okay. I'll think about it."

I felt like someone was
watching me just then.
Breeze? I didn't see her anywhere, though.
Strange.

73

SUNDAY—MORNING

An **explosion** shook me from sleep.

Mom and Dad were peeking out of their room at about the same time I was. Someone ran **by our house** shouting something about how we were **under attack.**

The west wall is **under attack.**
I hate weekends.
Really. I do.

Why does all the **crazy stuff** happen on weekends? I can't even remember the last time I had an **uneventful one.**

My father, of course, tried to **stop me.** Then he just sighed, nodded.

"I've realized by now that **I can't stop you** from going on your **crazy adventures,**" he said.

Mom smiled, although there was sadness in her eyes. "**My little warrior** is growing up so fast. Just be careful out there, all right?"

But they didn't have to **worry.** When I got to the west wall, I realized that it wasn't the **mobs** that had caused the explosion.

It was **some humans.** That's a new word I learned recently. *Human.* That's what they call themselves—**the people from Earth.** The west wall wasn't heavily fortified, so **their TNT** blasted through it pretty easily. When I got there, the humans **had already stepped through the hole** they'd created. About one hundred villagers were there, whispering to one another and studying **the two warriors.**

The warrior on the right pointed in our general direction. "You! Villagers! Is this Herobrine's castle?"

The mayor pushed through the crowd. "Herobrine?! We have nothing to do with the likes of him! Who are you, exactly?"

"I am Kolbert of the Lost Legion! I assumed this to be the Kingdom of Herobrine."

"Real sorry for that," said the other warrior, a girl, who introduced herself as Elisa. "Our clan is pushing eastward. We're trying to stop Herobrine's advance."

Lost Legion?
Never heard of them.

And what's a clan, anyway? I glanced at Max. The walking Wikipedia just shrugged. Moments later, the girl, Elisa, nudged Kolbert with an elbow.

"Right." Kolbert cleared his throat. "Ahem! This village is now under the control of the Lost Legion! As the clan's captain, I demand food, supplies, and shelter immediately!"

Murmurs swept through the crowd of villagers:

"What does he mean?"

"Why would we give them our stuff?"

"Is that guy crazy or something?"

"He means give them things?! For free?!"

"We will do no such thing!" the mayor said. "We have enough problems! Leave us alone!"

The two humans whispered to each other. Then Kolbert turned back to us. "You are NPCs!" he declared. "You will do as I say! You will kneel before us and show your respect!"

"Fail to assist us," Elisa said, "and we will lay siege to your village by sundown!"

The mayor glanced between the two of them.

"You and what army?"

Just then, more humans began to appear over a distant hill . . . and more . . . and more. There must have been over a hundred of them, and most of them looked *tough.* I mean, *tough.* Imagine a guy who's slept in a two-by-one cube emergency shelter in the ground for

77

months, eating bats and drinking rainwater. *(Two-by-one dimensions mean that you can't move your arms and you're sleeping upright.)* That's the kind of **tough** I'm talking about. Several of them, **like Kolbert, wielded diamond swords** and wore enchanted leather or iron armor.

"**Oh**," the mayor said. "Okay. **That army.** Well, come right in, then."

He opened the gate and let them all in. **A total of 125 humans, 88 horses, 31 donkeys, 17 cows,** and **11 dogs.** Oh. And **8 cats.** Also **3 chickens.** Also **a sheep. Yeah.** I am *not* drawing all of that.

So things are **even worse** in our village now. Now we can't even **walk** the streets without being harassed or bossed around in some way by a multitude of different people.

"**Hey! Villager!** Help me with this!"

"**Hey! Villager!** Help me with *that!*"

"**You! NPC!** Get over here and give us a hand!"

"You don't even know what **NPC** *means?!* That stands for **non-player character!**"

"NPC, that's what you are!"

"Sorry to break it to you kid, but you're just a **game** character! A bunch of computer data! **Oh,** don't cry! It's impossible for you to have feelings! **Hey!** I said **stop crying,** kid!"

"You exist only to **trade** with us!"

"We will **eat** your food!"

"We will **sleep** in your beds!"

"We will **barge into your house** whenever we want to, **open** your chests, mine part of your house, and possibly take your door."

"And also your **crafting table.**"

"And possibly your **furnace.**"

"And maybe the **carpet.**"

"Especially if it's white. I just love white carpeting."

"Blue's also **nice, though.**"

79

Emerald **didn't like being told what to do. Kolbert** demanded that she **clean** his new house for him. She **demanded** that he go **jump down a well** until his **air meter ran out. Surely you can see the problem here.** Call it a **personality clash.** The end result was . . . Emerald's **hands being tied behind her back** with **spider string.** She was then led to **Kolbert's** house, where she was untied and **forced to scrub the floors** on her hands and knees. **At swordpoint.** Here's **another problem:** Emerald is now a member of **Team Runt.**

I marched up to Kolbert. "I want you to release my friend."

"Who? The mouthy one?"

"That's right."

Kolbert turned to Elisa. "What's up with this village? Seriously. It's weird. Five-block-high cobblestone walls, hundreds of houses. One of them's even referring to himself as the mayor! And now we have villagers talking back and giving us orders."

The captain turned to me and pushed me back.

"Since you want to be with your friend so bad, how about you help her out?"

Just then, I saw Breeze drop down from a house into an alley to my right. She stepped out of the shadows.

"Release her," Breeze said.

Kolbert whirled around. "And who are you? Whatever. Looks like we'll have three workers, then." He took out some spider string and reached for Breeze.

"You really don't want to do that," I said.

81

The captain ignored my warning . . . and promptly found himself **facedown** in the grass.

Breeze had thrown **three punches** in **less than a second—** and these unarmed attacks **hit hard,** from what I could tell.

Kolbert rose, rubbing his cheek. "That girl," he said. "**She's . . . OP!!**" Breeze strode past him and stepped **into the house** that held Emerald.

"**These villagers are crazy!!**" Kolbert said.

"It could be **another player,**" Elisa said. "Maybe using some kind of **hack.**"

"**Maybe** . . . but if that's the case, we're talking **extensive skin hacks** here! I mean, what's up with the villager girls having **long hair** and **small noses?!**" He looked up to the sky. "**What is this place?!**"

"This is Minecraftia," Max said, approaching. "It's not a game. And we are not NPCs."

Stump stepped out from behind Max. "We will treat you with respect," he said, "but you must do the same. Got it?"

Kolbert nodded weakly.

"Well, good, then." Stump held out a cake. "Want a slice? Just made it."

And so this was the first step—one of many—toward getting the humans off our backs. At the end of the day, all five members of Team Runt went down to Snark's Tavern.

While we drank our tea, Breeze told me why she hadn't been in school last week.

"I was grounded," she said. "My father was really angry at me for joining the battle on Saturday. He said I shouldn't have risked my life like that . . ."

"Well, I owe you a big thanks," I said, "for that battle and today's. And . . . I'm super sorry for ignoring you before. Even if you really were the biggest noob, I'd still be your friend. Welcome to Team Runt!!"

83

She smiled. "Thanks."

"By the way," I said, "today, when you beat up Kolbert,
I didn't see you drinking any potions."

"Whatever. Let's have a feast, huh?"

The five of us ate and chatted for hours.
The way we joked around, it was as if the angry teachers,
the mob attacks, the rude humans,
and the constant threat of Herobrine . . .

it was as if all that wasn't
actually happening.

ONE WEEK LATER— SUNDAY, PART I

Oh, no.

Not this dream again.

What's up with that redstone machine, anyway?

Wait. What's an **enderman** doing in this dream?

"I . . . h-help you."

What? How can you help me?

"Another useless dream. Just your . . . fear."

I suppose you're controlling my dreams somehow? Endermen can do that?

"Oh, yes. Wait. Give you . . . g-good dream."

What's your name, anyway?

87

SAVE ME !!

C'mon, kid!
Get me out of here already!

You can't just ignore me forever, y'know! What, you are afraid of the Nether? The pigmen don't bite! Unless you bite them first . . . Say, tell ya what. You help me, and I'll tell ya where the secret treasure room is. I know where it is! I saw it! That'll serve 'em for abandoning me here . . . Besides, there's this kitten you really need to meet.

"By the way, you'd better wake up right now. Trust me on this one."

I woke up from the nightmare and climbed out of bed. When I looked out the window, the sky was bright red. Deep laughter echoed overhead. It was not unlike thunder.

Was I still dreaming?

"Dear?" My mom was in the living room, looking out the window. "What is that?"

"I don't know," I murmured.

I left my house after giving Mom **a worried glance.** It had to have been night still, or at least before sunrise, yet the red sky was so bright that it cast a fiery glow brighter than a full moon.

When I made my way to the fountain, **I spotted Max.** "What is this?"

He shrugged. Of course, there was no way he could explain what was going on. The **deep laughter** continued overhead as more and more villagers gathered at the square. **Members of the Legion** showed up as well. Kolbert looked **more** terrified than we were.

"Um . . . I'm guessing this isn't good," he said.

"Yeah," Emerald said. "I have to say, you guys kinda came at a really bad time."

"Stay calm, everyone!" The mayor weaved through the crowd and stood at the base of the fountain. "Go back inside! Seek shelter immediately!"

But everyone was staring at the sky. There was an eerie ringing sound, almost inaudible. More and more people, villagers and humans alike, moved closer to one another.

Mia and Mary embraced, their robes fanciful, their faces mournful.

"I'm gonna miss you, my BFF . . ."

"Hey! Don't talk like that, okay?! We're gonna be fine!!"

Moments later, Elisa tapped Kolbert on the shoulder. "You know, it's probably him."

The captain drew his sword. "Yeah, you're right. Man, he just won't leave us alone!"

"Who are you guys talking about?" Emerald asked.

"Herobrine, who else?"

"What? You mean he's *attacked you before?!*"

"Well, yeah. That's one of the reasons we're here."

Emerald approached him until she stood nose-to-nose with the captain. "Y'know, you might have *warned* us about that *before* we let you into our village!" She paused. "Wait. Where were you guys staying *before*?"

"Oh, well, we built a castle," Kolbert said.

"And what happened to it?"

"Well, um, basically . . . it was utterly destroyed."

Emerald grabbed him by the collar of his undershirt. "You . . ."

"D-don't worry!" Kolbert said. "Surely the same thing won't happen here! Your village is much, much bigger!"

Emerald sighed and pushed him away. "Jerk." Then she joined the rest of Team Runt. All five of us drew closer. Together, we gazed at the red sky.

Soon, a figure could be seen up there. It soared just below the clouds. More and more people noticed.

"Look!"

"Up there!"

"It's . . . a human!"

Then this person landed near the fountain. Indeed, it was a human. Or human-ish. An aura of godlike power emanated from him.

91

Even the **toughest-looking** Legion members—**in full iron armor, enchanted, with enchanted diamond swords**—**cowered** in fear.

It was the man I'd seen before **in a dream.** It was the **most powerful** wizard in this **world,** perhaps the very last. It was the wizard who went by the name of . . .

"Herobrine!!"

"It's **Herobrine!!**"

As some villagers **turned to run,** Herobrine raised a hand. A **chain of bluish-purple lightning** leaped from his fingertips and arced through the crowd. **I couldn't move.** I couldn't even speak. I **slumped** to one knee, **totally weak.** Everyone seemed to be affected in this way.

92

Then Herobrine's voice swept through the square:

"No matter how many mobs I send,
you just... won't... die!!"

This time, waves of red lightning flew from his hands and zapped everyone in the crowd.

I watched my health bar inch its way down. So Herobrine came to take care of us himself. Maybe it's because humans and villagers began cooperating.

Maybe that scared him.

I was barely able to turn my head to see Breeze, Brio, Drill, Stump, Max, or Kolbert... they were all in a similar condition. Herobrine raised his hand again, which would no doubt finish most of us off.

Just then,
another person
landed behind him—
fwump!

93

Like Herobrine, he had a powerful aura. Unlike Herobrine, however, there was something good about him, something peaceful and kind.

There was no doubt in my mind. It was Notch.

Herobrine whirled around. "It's been a while, old man. You've been spending way too much time on Earth."

Notch stepped forward. "Herobrine, you will stop this madness at once!"

"I'm afraid that's no longer possible," Herobrine said. "This is beyond my control now."

"So it's true? This world really is . . ." Notch looked down at his outstretched palms. "Tell me; how did you do it?"

"Even if I explained, you wouldn't understand."

"And why not?"

Herobrine turned away. "You always were one step behind . . ."

"Enough." Notch drew his sword—obsidian. "I don't know what you've done, but this will soon come to an end!"

There was a metallic whine as Herobrine drew his own sword, made of a metal I didn't recognize.

A thin smirk spread across his face.

94

"I'm not so sure of that."

When you looked at the two wizards facing off, all you could imagine was the most epic battle of all time. After all, if someone were to refer to them as the gods of this world, well . . . it wouldn't be an exaggeration.

Humans and villagers alike simply stood there in awe.

"Why do I get the feeling we're going to be repairing the village for weeks after this?" Emerald whispered.

How strange. I had that same feeling.

But the two wizards didn't fight. Not for very long, anyway. And at first they just kept talking.

"Put your sword away," Herobrine said. "We might be at war, but we're still gentlemen."

"That's funny, coming from you!" Notch said. "How many villages have you destroyed so far?"

"Only a few." Herobrine glanced around at the buildings. "I must say: they could have learned from these guys. At least they have walls."

At this, Notch growled and **swung his sword.** And that was it. The battle was on. **Obsidian** met **glowing red metal.** Sparks flew from Herobrine's blade.

By the way, these kinds of weapons were **common** ages ago. In ancient times, the mobs were a lot **stronger, different** from what we see now. You needed weapons like that just to **fight** some of them. Anything less and you **didn't stand a chance.** If we had weapons like that, we could cut through zombies like shears through cobwebs. **Sadly,** the crafting recipes have long since been forgotten . . .

"I believe Herobrine's sword is **elemental** in nature," Max said. **"Lava is one of the ingredients."**

"Can we make one?" I asked.

"I doubt it. We'd need a **special crafting table."**

Special crafting table? That was the first time I'd heard about something like that. But now was not the time for a crafting discussion.

Their blades **clashed** over and over again. At one point, Herobrine **hurled a green fireball,** which Notch deflected with his blade as one would deflect a ghast's.

96

"I see you've grown stronger," Notch said. "Or maybe you've become soft." Their blades met once more. Their faces were inches apart. Herobrine smiled. "Yes, I think you've been spending way too much time on Earth!"

"Say what you want!" Notch said. "You won't be speaking much longer!"

"No, I'm afraid it is you who won't be speaking. I tire of this."

Suddenly, Herobrine stepped back, and pink lightning flew out from his free hand.

It zapped Notch . . . and the wizard became . . . a black rabbit.

For a moment, it was as if time itself had stopped. At least for me. I just couldn't believe what I was seeing. One of the greatest wizards of all time—a legendary hero—defeated, just like that.

We'd learned in school that Notch was the only one capable of stopping this madman. The only one powerful enough. But Herobrine had turned him into a helpless animal with no effort at all. Which meant . . . this war was over.

We were history.

Behind me, a girl **screamed.** There were a few gasps here and there. The humans talked excitedly among themselves:

"He . . . **polymorphed** Notch?!"

"Was that some kind of **admin command?**"

"So, like, we have to fight him ourselves or something?"

"A **boss battle?!** I'm in!!"

"I wonder how much **life** he has . . ."

"**Who cares?!** Imagine the experience!!"

"And the **loot!** I hope **he drops** that sword . . . !!"

There were a lot of comments like these. It seemed most of the humans had no idea how much **danger** they were in . . . It was almost as if they were expecting Herobrine to say,

"Just kidding! Trolled ya!
This is a **new version** of the game!
The latest in virtual reality! Pretty amazing, right?"

Herobrine picked up the rabbit and stroked its neck. He did so with a slight grin. He was obviously proud of his work. When he turned to the crowd, you couldn't help but stare into his glowing white eyes . . .

"People of Earth," he said, his voice impossibly loud, "welcome . . . to Minecraftia. Please understand: I'm not the one who brought you here. Thank him for that." He looked down at his new pet. "He summoned you in one last, pathetic attempt to stop me."

The mayor emerged from the crowd. "If I may ask . . . why did you come here?"

"I came to make an offer. For the humans, I'm willing to send you all back. You will return to Earth, safe and sound, with almost no memory of this world. You will wake up thinking that this was all . . . just a dream. As for the villagers, your lives will be spared. You'll be able to go on farming and building, just like you always have. Of course, in return, you must do something for me."

99

Kolbert, the **leader of the humans,** joined the mayor up front.

"Forget it!" He drew his sword. "The Legion does not negotiate with boss monsters! You are a **walking pile of experience orbs** to us!

Nothing more!"

Herobrine **chuckled. "Oh? You must think you're still in his little game.** How sad. **He never told you anything, did he?"**

Kolbert opened his mouth again.

But before he replied, **Brio's men** grabbed him.

"What is this?!" the knight shouted. "The players should be making the decisions!! **Not you NPCs!!"**

"Forgive this human!" the mayor said. "He's a bit confused, you see. Anyway, **we're willing to cooperate! What do you want from us?!"**

A lot of people, both humans and villagers, gave the mayor a **confused** look. I was one of them.

There was a **long silence.** Herobrine's gaze swept across the crowd. Then a banner appeared in his other hand. **It was white** with a strange **black symbol** in the middle. Herobrine tossed it onto the street.

100

"I . . . . want you to surrender."

Surrender.

It took a second for me to understand what he just said. Everyone around me was equally shocked. Breeze moved closer to me. Even she was scared. Although Herobrine didn't smile, I somehow knew that he was enjoying watching us squirm.

"Place this banner in a visible location," he said, "and my mobs will not harm you. Some will live in your village. You will supply them with the materials they need. In addition, you will help them improve their farming and building techniques."

"And how do we know you'll keep your word?" the mayor asked.

"You can ask Urf. I'll tell him to pay a little visit. As a general in my army, he has everything he's ever wanted. Power. Money. Respect. All these things can be yours as well, if you just kneel before me . . . and accept me as your king. You have two weeks to decide. That is when my main army will arrive at your gates. If they do not see that banner, believe me when I say that there will be nothing left of this place—and nothing left of you."

The more he talked, the quieter we became. But there were still a few whispers here and there.

"Urf!"

"That traitor!"

"So he's some kind of boss monster, now?"

So Herobrine wanted us to give up. Not only that, he wanted us to join him?! It was unimaginable. Humans and villagers working with mobs. Kolbert was right—how could we do such a thing? How could the mayor agree? But then, the mayor was only looking out for us. He would do anything he could to protect us. Even if that meant . . .

No!

We can't do that!

I pushed to the front and shouted:

"If you're asking for our help, that means you're afraid of the villages to the west! Some of them are even bigger than this one! You've realized you haven't been able to defeat us, and you'll have an even harder time dropping them!"

I honestly don't know what came over me. When I said all that, I . . . felt like a different person. Someone strong and brave.

This seemed to get Herobrine's attention. He stared at me. He seemed to be thinking about something.

"How interesting," he said. "Tell me: who are you?"

"I am Runt Ironfurnace," I said.

"And I'm asking you to surrender."

Yeah. I actually said that. Seriously, what was I thinking? I wasn't thinking, I guess—just angry.

"Shut up! Shut up!" The mayor said this through clenched teeth.

Herobrine made the most ridiculous face. Imagine a creeper smiling as if it had just heard that cats had become extinct—it was something like that. Then he laughed so hard that if he really had been a creeper, he probably would have exploded. But then the laughter abruptly stopped. His smile faded, replaced by an expression of extreme irritation, as if the street beneath his feet was made of slime blocks instead of cobblestone.

"You will join me!" he cried. "You will help me restore this world to its—"

The rabbit jumped out of Herobrine's arms. Then it began **shaking** on the ground until a **puff of smoke** obscured it. The smoke faded, revealing a **very angry Notch.**

"**Don't listen to him!**" he shouted. "If he ruled the **Overworld,** it would make the Nether look like a mushroom island!"

Herobrine glared at him. *"How did you break out of my spell?!"*

But Notch was no longer **in the mood** for conversation. There was a sharp ringing sound as their blades met once more. This time, Notch moved with the **strength of an iron golem** and the speed of a mine cart on powered rails.

Herobrine struggled to keep up. He dashed back. *"No matter what you do, you can't stop me! In two weeks, unless they join me, this place will be in ruins! The west will crumble next!"*

With that, **he suddenly flew up into the sky.**

This world is **mine.**

Notch turned to us. He didn't say anything for a second or two. Even though it wasn't a very long time, it felt like forever. When he finally spoke, the expression on his face could have made a ghast look happy.

"Build, you fools!"

That was it. That was all he said. It meant fortify the village. It meant prepare for the next attack. Without another word, he took off into the sky. He was chasing Herobrine. Before long, the two of them had vanished into the clouds.

Everyone just stared upward. The humans were too confused about what had just happened. Some had the most clueless expressions. Some of them might have been great players back home, but here, they didn't understand a thing. As for us villagers . . . well, most of us were too scared to speak or even move. Finally, Elisa, the Legion sub-leader, joined Kolbert and the mayor.

"So, um, now what?" she asked.

"What do you mean?!" the mayor snapped. "We build, just like he said!"

Kolbert nodded. "I never thought I'd ever agree with an NPC, but yes—we won't give in to the likes of him!"

105

"We will fight to the last noob and villager!!"

Another human named Minsur raised his sword. "Yeahhhh!! The Legion doesn't know defeat!!"

Steve and Mike looked at each other in a glum way.

"Everyone meet at the city hall!" the mayor shouted. "We can't just stand around! Notch is up there fighting for us at this very moment!

"We are at war!"

SUNDAY—PART II

At city hall, while we waited for the **mayor** to start speaking, **everyone was talking about what had happened.**

Notch this.

Herobrine that.

Their magic was so cool!

Are we really going to surrender?

Does anyone know how to **craft the sword** *Herobrine was using?*

(That last question was mine. Tee-hee. Of course, no one knew how.)

My heart had **stopped pounding** by then. I expected more to happen, honestly . . . but seeing Notch break out of the **polymorph spell** had been pretty cool. *(Herobrine's lightning, ehhhhhh, not so cool. It hurt. A lot. If that's what charged creepers have to go through, I almost feel sorry for them.)*

The mayor finally spoke. "First, let me say that I don't believe we should **surrender.** I just didn't want him to hurt anyone."

"You mean we're actually going to **fight back?**" a girl asked. That was **Sophia,** someone on **Team All Girls.**

107

"Herobrine seems so strong," her friend Emma said. "How can we possibly defeat him?"

"We've faced many hardships before," the mayor said. "Humans in the form of griefers, trolls, and noobs. Mobs who have grown ever smarter—who use tactics like creeper bombs and zombie ladders. But soon we will face our biggest threat: Herobrine himself. As we understand, his main army is stronger than anything we've seen so far."

"How do you know, sir?" That was Pebble. He was in the front row. The mayor's little pet.

His buddy, Rock, joined in: "Your excellency, have you seen his army?"

"I haven't," the mayor said. "But . . . there are some who have."

The mayor turned to Brio and then stepped away from the wooden block he'd been standing behind. Brio took his place and gazed into the crowd.

"Please come up," Brio said. At first I thought he was speaking to me. But then I realized, no . . . he was talking to someone right next to me. Breeze.

108

She glanced at Stump, Max, Emerald, and me, then pushed her way through the crowd. Stump and I looked at each other with expressions that said, "What in the Nether is going on?!"

"For those of you who don't know me," Brio said, "I am the mayor's head assistant. I haven't lived in your village for very long. I come from a village to the east of here, near Herobrine's castle. And this—"

He put his arm around Breeze.

"—is my daughter."

Wow.

Wowowowow.

109

So that **explains a lot**. Everyone around me was totally **freaking out,** but they stopped as soon as Brio continued. "Over a year ago, our village was **attacked,**" he said. "Many lives were lost that day. However, my daughter and I, we . . . we were **captured.** Even then, the mobs were **under Herobrine's control.** They took us to his castle, where we were **held prisoner.** And Herobrine, he . . ."

Brio looked downward.

"He **experimented** on us."

When I heard this, his words were flint and steel and my mind was a block of **TNT—my mind was BLOWN.** Breeze, **the silent girl. The weird girl.** The girl a lot of kids whispered about.

Herobrine had **tried** to turn her into some kind of super-soldier?! What kind of **experiments** did he do?!

I was **so curious** . . . but Brio answered before I could even ask.

"He **infused us with magic,**" he said. "The same way one enchants a tool or a piece of armor, he . . . **enchanted** us."

To my right, Stump gasped. "So that **explains their purple eyes.** That's why Brio wears **sunglasses!** That's why Breeze hides her face with her **hair!**"

110

"Man," Emerald said, "what did Herobrine do? Throw them onto an enchanting table like they were items or something?"

"I remember reading something about that in the ancient texts," Max said.

As Breeze stood next to her father, she lowered her head as well.

I felt so sorry for her. She must have felt like an outsider. A freak. It explained so much. Why she was so quiet and . . . why she was so strong.

"While we were held prisoner, we overheard many things," Brio said. "We learned that the purpose of his experiments was to create an army stronger than anything this world has ever seen. But villagers are good at heart. No matter how much he tried, he couldn't control our minds. Before long, we managed to escape. Our village was in ruins by then, so we moved west . . . and found yours."

I noticed a tear running down Breeze's cheek—it looked like a small glass square. Whatever she had experienced back then, it must have been horrible.

"And there you have it," the mayor said. "This is what we're dealing with, folks. An army of

111

magically enhanced mobs—we're not talking about a random group of **potion-chugging, helmet-wearing zombies** this time. Please forgive me for not telling you sooner. I simply didn't want to **cause a panic.** In the end, you can feel safe knowing that we have people here who have actually seen **Herobrine's castle** with their own eyes. They know what we're dealing with."

Many villagers nodded to each other.

There were many *hurrrs* and *hurms* and *rhurrrggs.*

"So everyone put your **tryhard** pants on," Brio said. "We all have to do our part. We all have to do extra chores now. Even you, students. No more games on the weekends. No more hanging out at the fountain after school. This village is going to become an **efficient, mob-slaying, redstone machine.** And you are just one of its many redstone circuits."

Many students groaned.

"Aw, man. **Wars are so lame.**"

"**This isn't fair!** I was supposed to go fishing this afternoon!"

112

"If this village is a redstone machine," Emerald said, "I'm a repeater, not a circuit."

"Extra chores?! I already have so much homework!" The girl who shouted this glanced back up at the sky. "I really hate you, Herobrine!!"

An old man simply asked, "Ehh? What are 'tryhard pants'?"

(For the record, my tryhard pants are ALWAYS on. I NEVER take them off.)

SUNDAY—PART III

So like the mayor said, everyone must **work constantly.** With the threat of a **huge mob invasion,** there's simply no more time for anything else. That includes getting ice cream, which is something my friends and I almost **always** do on Sunday afternoons.

So annoying.

Herobrine, you're **messing up** my schedule, **man!**

School, school, school.
Chores, chores, chores.

Will there ever be a time when it's just **play, play, play?** I should look at the bright side, though: after this, Pebble will probably be **way too tired** to harass me much.

Speaking of Pebble . . .

I was standing in line with Stump, Emerald, and Max. We were waiting to get our assigned **chores.** And Team Pebble was a little ways behind us in line. I heard Pebble say, "If a bunch of endermen attack, **all**

114

we need to do is send Runt at them. He cries so much he's like a walking fountain! No enderman would get within twenty blocks of him!"

A bunch of kids laughed. It got worse, though. Soon after that, the mayor approached Pebble. "I want you to make some more posters. You are excused from doing chores. Have you and your friends come to my house."

"Nice! Thank you, your excellency!"

Wow.

I guess being a war hero really has its perks. Pebble shoved me out of the way as he passed me. "Later, noobling," he said. "Work hard for me, huh?"

Sap, Donkey, and Sara smirked as they walked by.

Rock winked at me. "Enjoy your chores."

Then the mayor called Emerald and Breeze over. They were going to make their own posters, the mayor said. After all, in her own way, Breeze is an actual war hero. She survived whatever Herobrine had done to her.

"What about our friends?" Emerald asked, pointing to the rest of Team Runt.

115

Breeze glanced at me. "Can they come with us, too?"

"Afraid not," the mayor said. "Girls only. I want the other girls to see that they can be strong too!"

Emerald and Breeze nodded and waved good-bye to us.

"Sorry, guys," Emerald said. "I tried."

Breeze looked sad. "I'll come help you when I can."

Watching them go, I felt so jealous. Especially when I listened to the chores Drill and Brio were giving the rest of us kids. They all sounded so terrible . . .

First, there was the slopper. That's someone who has to craft mushroom stew, over and over. Our village has a lot of extra mushrooms. They're not really used for anything except stew. So the mayor said that we should all try to eat mushroom stew as much as possible and save all the other food for when things get really bad.

I don't understand the logic behind this. (Remember that villagers are strange sometimes. Before Steve showed up, we hadn't even thought about building a wall. A WALL. How sad is that?)

Then there were the sorters. They have to organize the contents of chests in the village supply rooms. That doesn't sound bad, until you think about what kind of items they handle. Spider eyes. Rotten zombie flesh. Slimeballs. Bones. Oh, and gunpowder, which is basically a creeper's innards.

The repairers work with the sorters. They go around the village finding two of the same item with low durability and combine them to take advantage of the 5% repair bonus. Some of the most common items that need repairing are leather boots—I'm guessing most of these unlucky kids will end up smelling like feet.

Hurrggg.

There were a lot of chores like that. That was why, when it was finally my turn to be assigned, I was silently praying to Notch: Please don't let my chores have anything to do with mushroom stew.

It didn't look good, though. Drill was the one assigning me.

He grinned. "Hello, Runt. Ya wanna hear the good news or the bad news first?"

"Good news, please."

"All right. You'll be working with Stump."

117

Wow.

That was good news.

Ridiculously good news.

The best possible news ever.

(Well, maybe not the best. He could have said something like, "Your job will be tasting cookies to ensure their quality and freshness.")

Still, I wasn't complaining at all. In fact, I cheered and gave my best friend a high-five. (By the way, Steve said that in the original game the villagers didn't have fingers. But here they do. They're blocky, though. Steve said our fingers look like big French fries. I'm not sure if that's good or bad. And hey, if it's bad, well . . . in this world, his fingers look just the same!)

I looked at Drill fearfully. ". . . and the bad news?" I asked.

(No mushroom stew. No mushroom stew. No mushroom stew. Please, please, please, please, please . . .)

The combat teacher grinned even more. "In three hours, your arms will know the true meaning of the word 'pain.'"

He handed each of us a stone axe.

At least it wasn't some wooden bowls.

SUNDAY—PART IV

Before, when I thought about fighting mobs in a war, I imagined dropping **a mountain of zombies.**

I imagined **diamond swords** and high-level enchantments.

I imagined people **cheering my name.**

Not this.

I hate this job . . . uh . . . **birches**.

119

Yeah. **We're choppers.** That's a fancy word for **lumberjack.** You see, the village needs **more arrows.** Enough to fill **five double chests.** That was why Drill ordered Stump and me to go to the **tree farm.** *(The place where I first met Breeze.)*

So starting today, we go to school **every morning.** Then, when school's over, we don't head home. We **must chop trees. So many trees.**

"Why do birch trees have to be **so tall?**" I asked.

That's the **annoying** part of harvesting wood. There's always that **last block** you can't quite reach. So you need to throw down a wood block from your inventory and jump on top of it. Then after harvesting the once unreachable block, you have to harvest the other block **a second time.**

I almost wished I was an **enderman.** Stump finished chopping his own block and **wiped sweat** from his brow. "It could be worse," he said.

"**Yeah? How?**"

"We could be doing this on **Earth.** Mike once said the trees there **fall over** after being chopped."

"**Seriously?**"

"That's what he said. And when they do, the lumberjacks shout, '**Timber!**'"

120

"What does that mean?"

"I have no idea. Anyway, let's be thankful we're here, huh? At least the trees won't squash us."

"Good point."

Man, Earth really is a strange place. Some of the people in my village say that Earth is just a myth. When I hear about things like trees that fall to the ground, I almost want to agree with them. I mean, come on. Falling trees? Who could believe that? There's no way that could possibly be true . . .

I soon finished chopping another block. I let out a huge breath. "You know, it really is quiet out here."

"Yeah . . ." Stump glanced at the surrounding trees. "It's almost like we really are . . . out there."

Out there. He meant beyond the wall. Even though the tree farm looks like wilderness, it's near the center of the village. I picked up an oak sapling that had fallen from the leaves overhead.

"This is what it would be like." I planted the sapling in the grass at my feet. "To be a warrior, I mean. A real one, like Steve. All alone. No one around for thousands of blocks. No one else to rely on but yourself."

121

"I dreamed I was outside once," Stump said. "I had a log house in the woods. I went out to explore and got lost. The sun was going down, and I couldn't find the way back. I panicked after that. I started running. The forest was getting darker and darker and my house was nowhere in sight. I couldn't even see torchlight. And I wasn't sure if I was getting closer or moving farther away . . ."

After he told me this, the forest suddenly seemed so scary. We drew closer to each other. Both of us looked around with wide eyes.

"Sounds more like a nightmare." I paused. "You know, someday, if we ever become warriors, the mayor might actually send us . . . out there."

My friend swallowed nervously. "You mean, like scouts?"

"Maybe. I heard the elders talking about it the other day."

"I guess that makes sense. We need to know what's going on out there."

"Exactly."

We chatted like this for a while. It was honestly like the good old days, back before I started this diary. Back when I thought Herobrine was just a fairy tale. Back when the mobs weren't so clever. Back then, Stump and I often went to places like this and just talked and

122

talked about **anything and everything**. So even though today came with a lot of hard work, **it wasn't all bad.**

For at least **an hour** today, we totally forgot about **the war.** The mobs. The two wizards. The possibility of our village being **utterly destroyed.** While we swung our axes and talked about random stuff, it was like we were innocent kids again. But eventually we had to come back to reality. **It was something that couldn't be ignored.** You just couldn't avoid it. These days, you can't get a **cup of tea** in my village without hearing about Herobrine at least **fifty times.** He's trying to **take over the world** . . . with a huge **army** of mobs . . . and there's almost no one left to fight him. There's **Notch,** sure. A handful of villages in the west, **yeah.** And then there's this village . . . with **tryhard noobs** like myself . . . and **a bunch of clueless humans.**

"I wonder if the wars in the past were **the same** as this one," I said.

Stump shook his head. "There were **a lot more people** back then."

"I guess you're right."

I thought back, recalling what **Mr. Beetroot** had taught us in history class the other day . . .

123

Long ago, this world was once filled with **all kinds** of people. There were people who were **part wolf** . . . others who were **half pig** . . . even people who looked **like the humans** from Earth.

There were **kings** and **princesses, valiant knights** who slew the fiercest mobs . . . merchants, scholars, wizards, thieves, and everything in between.

But now,
there is nothing.

When you look at **my world** now, it's mostly wilderness—**an endless amount** of grass blocks, dirt blocks, stone, sand, and water blocks. These **simple cubes** form hills, mountains, deserts, valleys, rivers, lakes, forests, swamps, plains, chasms. But when it comes to civilization, my world doesn't have much to offer. Every **now and then,** you might spot a village. That's all that remains. It's hard to imagine that those lands once contained towns and cities, castles—**vast kingdoms.** Knowing that, one must ask . . . where did all the people go?

Simple. They **vanished** in **puffs of smoke** long ago. Back then there was **a huge war** led by Herobrine. In this first war, the various

124

races joined together and drove the mobs back. They even defeated Herobrine. But he didn't die. He retreated into some underground lair where he plotted his revenge for many, many years.

Much later, he launched a second war. It was way worse than the first. He still lost that war . . . but every kingdom, city, and castle was destroyed. So many lives were lost defending them. Entire races were wiped out. Remember when I said one of those wolf people visited our village once? He's the only wolf man we've ever seen. We believe he's the last one left. He hasn't shown up in months. Maybe the mobs got him, too.

Stump and I talked about this, but we found it depressing and a little boring. We soon changed the topic to something far more interesting. Magic.

"How cool would it be to actually cast a spell?" I said.

Stump nodded. "Shoot fireballs like a blaze . . ."

"Teleport like an enderman."

"Summon a kitten just before a creeper gets close to you . . ."

"Whoa. Can wizards actually do that?"

He shrugged. "Why not? If they can bring humans here, they can surely summon kittens."

"Hurmmm. I never considered that."

"I wonder whether a wizard can create food, then?"

"Well, if they can summon kittens, maybe they can summon cake, too?"

"I wish I could do that." He sighed. "Would make my life so much easier."

When he said this, I thought of something. All this time, I've wanted to become a warrior . . . But what about becoming a wizard? How crazy would that be, huh?

I pushed this ridiculous idea away. As far as I knew, no village had ever had wizards before. I'd heard stories of some who turned evil and became witches—but even then, they just dabbled in potions, not actual spells.

Stump gave me a funny look. "Hey, you're awfully quiet all of a sudden," he said. "What are you thinking about?"

I smiled and shook my head.

I chopped at some more wood.

"Nothing, dude. Nothing."

SUNDAY—PART V

After chopping for **over an hour,** our inventories were nearly filled up. I felt like an **expert lumberjack.** Swing **this way** and **that way**—I know how to **chop!** Pebble had better **pray** that the village doesn't have a wood-chopping competition!

I'll be there for that!
I'll be the **first** one to sign up!

With all of that chopping, our **hunger bars** had gotten pretty low. So we took a **break.** As usual, Stump had brought some cake. Steve once said eating in this world is just like **in the game.** No matter how carefully you eat, crumbs go flying. But then, I'm never careful. Why should I be? A warrior should **eat quickly.** If I'm ever in battle and need to top off my hunger bar, do you think I can just **call time out?!**

Ahem. *Excuse me, my dear zombies. May we take a break from all this fighting?* **My hunger bar,** *you see . . . . allow me to set a dinner table so that I may replenish it. You're most welcome to join me. We shall have an appetizer followed by a main course and then a most elegant dessert.*

127

As if.

No, that food needs to be eaten as quickly as possible so my health bar can **regenerate** in combat! Sword in one hand, half-eaten cookie in the other—that's a **real warrior!** So today, during our break, when I jammed a whole slice of cake in my mouth, I wasn't being a pig—no, no, no. I was just . . . **training.** Yeah. Training. **That's it.**

"**Oh,** I almost forgot," I said. "I bought you **some robes** just like mine. They've been in my inventory the whole time."

I handed him the robes, **the special boots,** and **the mask.** He slipped into them immediately, then looked down at himself.

"**Hurrmmm.** These robes are **really cool** and all, but . . . we look kind of similar now, **don't we?**"

He was right. Our robes were the same **dark gray color.**

"Emerald did mention that these robes can be dyed," I said.

"**Oh.**" Stump turned his gaze to the woods. "I guess we're in luck, then."

Yes, we were in luck. The tree farm has just as many flowers as it does trees. All we had to do was go around and pick whatever color we needed.

128

"I wanna dye my robes black," Stump said. "I wanna look just like Notch!! All black with an obsidian sword. Even a big hat!"

"You need ink, then. Not flowers. We can go squid hunting in the pond. Wait. Maybe we should think about this carefully."

"Why?"

"Well, Emerald came up to me the other day . . ."

I told Stump about what Emerald had said about popularity and how we're not exactly on many people's friend lists.

"Tomorrow at school, let's ask all the other kids what their favorite color is," I said. "We'll dye our robes the two most popular colors. That's sure to boost our popularity, right?"

Stump looked unsure about this idea. "I dunno . . . what if most of them like rust brown or something?"

"That's the risk we take!" I said. "Our team needs more allies!"

"All right." His uncertainty seemed to fade. "Let's do this."

MONDAY—PART I

Remember that time Razberry distracted me by asking **a bunch of random questions?** At school I kinda felt like him today. We just went up to kids and asked, **"What's your favorite color?"**

Or, **"What color do you like most?"**

And also, "If you were stuck on a deserted island **with just one color,** what color would that be?"

As you can imagine, we got a lot of **weird looks.** Still, when we show up at school in our dyed robes, it'll be **totally worth it.**

Here are the totals.

- Gray: 2
- Obsidian: 3
- Blue: 29
- Red: 23
- Orange: 4
- Purple: 3

- Black: 20
- Green: 17
- Yellow: 1
- Pink: 1
- White: 2
- Greenish-yellowish brown: 1

We lumped **similar colors** into one category. For example, a few said **lapis lazuli** was their favorite color—we counted that as **blue.**

130

Obviously, blue was the clear winner, followed by **red.** We dyed the robes after school on the tree farm. It took us only about **five minutes** to gather enough **blue orchids** and **poppies.** We didn't even need a crafting table. *(Not that we were short on wood or anything.)*

Well,

what do you think?

Watch out, Herobrine! This will be the last thing you see.

The first person I showed off my new robes to was Breeze. I ran into her after I came back from the tree farm.

"**I like that color,**" she said. "It's somehow **peaceful.**"

131

Of course, I asked her what it was like being a **prisoner** in Herobrine's castle. She shared her **experiences** there but made me promise not to write about it. I wouldn't have written about it even if she hadn't. You'd probably start **crying** if you knew what the mobs did to her. **I almost did.** The thought of eating grass stew for weeks and weeks . . . how could the mobs be **so cruel?!**

Oops.
Please forget I wrote that.
(Breeze would get angry, and I'd rather face Herobrine than her.)

In the end, I **reassured** her that we're good friends—and that she'll always be a part of **Team Runt.** I also said, since we're such good friends, she should tell me how Herobrine managed to make her **so strong.**

She wouldn't **tell me.**
She claimed she **didn't know.**

Whatever. I'm about to go to an enchanting house and sleep on an enchanting table myself.

Wish me **luck.**

MONDAY—PART II

Well, I just took a nap on an enchanting table. And when I did, I learned something very important.

Enchanting tables are very, very uncomfortable. In other words, nothing happened. I feel like I've been scammed! I just want to be able to kick a zombie so hard it flies back thirty blocks. At least thirty. Is that too much to ask?!

Hurrmmmph!

After my chores were done, I visited Max at the library. He'd been assigned to rearrange all the books. At least this suited him.

"Did you say that you've read something about people being enchanted?" I asked.

He closed some random book.

"Yes. It's done through something called a rune chamber."

"What's that?"

133

"It's like an enchanting table for **pets.** Let's say you had a pet wolf. You could place the wolf in this chamber and give it **special powers.**"

"Like what?"

"**Like,** you could give its bite a **knockback effect** or a **flame effect** or **increase its armor.** I guess you could do this with any pet, even baby ones."

"So maybe **Herobrine** figured out a way for this table to enchant people?"

"**Maybe.** I need to keep researching."

"Good. Let me know what you **find out.**"

I know, I know. So many bad things are happening in my village. All you really need to know is . . . **Herobrine is a punk.** Take Pebble. Multiply his bad attitude by ten. Give him the ability **to cast crazy spells.** Now you have Herobrine, the **Ultimate Bad Guy.**

To think, I **actually mouthed off to him!** He's gonna be looking out for me now! I may have to **change my name.**

I shouldn't have shared my problems with you. If you weren't crying before, you must be crying now. "Oh, those poor, poor villagers," you're probably saying between sobs. "Won't they ever get a break?!"

If you're reading this and you're a ghast, please come to my house!

Your tears will go for a fortune here!
We can start a very profitable business together!

Well, our **idea** paid off. It could just be my imagination, but the other kids treated me **better** at school today. At least I'm not getting so many dirty looks.

But having **nice robes** is just one part of the equation.
When I get a chance,
I need to ask **Emerald** more about that.

Before classes even started, Brio informed us that there are **two tests** coming up. One is the **mining test.** It had been delayed for some reason. So we're having that next week. The other test is **a building test.** Each group must come up with a new way to protect our village. **Cactus** pits. **Lava** moats. **Piston** traps that crush mobs into goo. Yeah! We're finally getting to the **cool stuff!** After school, I'm gonna spend all day dreaming up such things.

Oh. Wait. I have no time to think about all that! I have way **too many trees** to chop after school! I've already crafted **an iron axe.** And now I'm thinking about using up some of my experience points to enchant it. That's how **serious** I am about my chores. In fact, I'm so serious **about harvesting wood** I'm even thinking about putting two axes on my hotbar. First, there will be the iron axe—the basic axe I normally use. Then there will be a gold axe—for when I need to chop **really, really fast.** As I said, you will never see a more serious harvester of wood. After I'm done harvesting a block, I will Immediately turn to the next block and begin chopping all over again. After school, so many trees will be chopped. After school, we will be the most professional woodchoppers in the **Overworld,** the **Nether,** the **End,** and even **the Void.**

After school,
there will be absolutely no <u>**goofing around.**</u>

Stump tried to chop the oak tree with his stone sword.
It didn't really work.

"Overlord Runt!" he shouted. "This oak golem is way too tough!"

"Then we must surround it!" I shouted back.

"Of course, my lord!"

138

We were standing next to each other, so there was no reason for us to be shouting. We were just doing that for **dramatic effect.** We were also trying to sound like **courageous knights.** However, our dialogue was **a little cheesy** . . .

Stump dashed to the other side of the "**oak golem.**" "Take this, **foul** tree mob!!"

Meanwhile, I stabbed the golem from the front. "You're right, **Commander Stump!** This golem's bark is like **enchanted bedrock armor!**"

"Perhaps we should use **magic!**" Stump took out a water bucket from his inventory. "**Frost II!**"

He dumped the bucket of water next to the oak tree—err, the oak golem.

"**Great work!**" I said. "The frost has frozen its feet! **Now it can't move!**"

"Do oak golems even have feet?"

"Who cares? **Attack,** Commander Stump! **Attack!!**"

"At once, sir!"

We began clobbering the tree from both sides with our swords.

"**Hurrggg!!** You'll never take our village!!"

"We are wizards and warriors, **leaf head!!**"

139

"There will be nothing left of you but **planks!!**"

So we weren't really fighting an oak golem. We were just making the best of our lumberjack situation. Can you blame us? As we finished off the **legendary** tree monster . . . there was a laugh in the distance. A girl's laugh.

It was Emerald.

"What are you guys doing?" she called out.

Stump and I froze in place. We slowly turned our heads to her, then back at each other, then back to Emerald again.

I lowered my sword. "Umm . . ."

"**Well,** we were just, **uh** . . . testing out how fast stone swords can **harvest wood,**" Stump said.

"**Yeah?** And why is there water everywhere?"

Oh. Right. We were standing knee-deep in water from Stump's bucket. Stump scooped the spring back up, but the damage was already done. **Soggy boots are no fun.**

Emerald rolled her eyes. "You guys are such **noobs.**"

I decided to change the topic quickly. "What are you doing out here, **anyway?**"

She looked at me as if I'd just asked whether **ender dragons** really fly.

"Drill wanted me to check on you guys," she said. "I mean, **hello?** The sun's going down in **an hour.**"

She was right. The blue sky was already beginning to take on a golden tinge just above the trees. It would be night soon. Even so, we would be **safe** out here at night. Torches covered every block of this tree farm with light. There was no chance that any mobs could spawn even in this secluded area. But when Herobrine's influence can be felt everywhere . . . even your own bedroom **seems scary,** let alone a place like this.

We headed back. I hadn't seen Breeze at all today, so I asked how she was doing.

"She's all right," Emerald said. "I've been trying to get her to be a little more **outgoing.**"

I turned to her and said something boring and lame, like, "**That's good.**"

That was when I **noticed** it.
In the distance, past Emerald, there was a
hole in the ground.

This hole was about as hard to find as Breeze. At night. During heavy rain.

"What are you **staring at?**" Then Emerald saw it too. "**Um,** were you guys **trying to test** how well swords dig holes?"

Stump and I **shook our heads** wordlessly. It was a **terrifying** discovery. A hole had been **dug** in the tree farm. Grass grew around it, helping to **hide it from view.** I only spotted it by chance when I'd glanced at Emerald.

We soon **learned** that it
was more than just a hole.

It had **a ladder** along one side that went down several blocks.

It was . . . **a tunnel.**

What's the big deal?
It's probably just
some guy's house.
A guy with
blue skin, eight
legs, and super
venomous fangs.

"I don't believe this," Stump said. "The mobs have been digging right under our village?"

143

I looked both of my friends in the eye. "Either that, or **Urf** made this. Or maybe there's another **traitor** we don't know about."

"Well, we've gotta go tell the mayor," Emerald said.

I carefully **approached the edge of the hole** and peered in. "How about we solve this **mystery** on our own? I mean, if there really is another **spy** in our village, they could be close to the mayor. So if we do the right thing and report it . . . maybe the spy will come and **cover** it all up."

"**I agree,**" Stump said. "Besides, I don't want someone else taking credit for our discovery."

"Maybe we're getting ahead of ourselves," Emerald said. "This could be something that **Steve guy made.**"

"Then maybe we should check," I said.

"**We'?**"

As Emerald said this, Stump gave me **a pitiful look.** Of course. I didn't **even bother arguing.**

Torch in one hand, I climbed down the **ladder.** The shaft ended after five blocks. **The floor was cobblestone.** As I'd expected, it didn't lead to a **storeroom** or anything like that.

144

The tunnel went straight for as far as the eye could see . . . which, um, wasn't very far.

A small part of me wanted to **explore,** just to see how far it went. *(The rest of me was trembling and sweating uncontrollably.)* I climbed **back up** and told my friends about it and how it was **heading east.**

"Of course it's heading east," Stump said. "It probably leads to the mob's forest."

"**Great,**" Emerald said. "So the **mobs made a tunnel.** If we're not gonna report it, **then what?**"

145

"I say we wait," said Stump. "Maybe we can find out who's using it."

"And how are we gonna do that?" Emerald demanded.

Stump glanced upward.
I followed his gaze
to the top of a tree.

Oh, look! There isn't a ladder on this tree! Good, well, we tried. There's nothing else to do.

"Move over! You guys are such tree hogs!"

Yeah. We totally climbed a tree. We also removed some of the leaves to make a nice, little hiding spot. If spies were using that tunnel, they would probably use it at night, right? All we had to do was wait and listen. Eventually, the spy would come. That was Stump's thinking, anyway. It made sense.

Emerald's stomach grumbled. "Man . . . I really need to remember to keep some food in my inventory."

Stump handed her a slice of cake. She almost took a bite, then stopped. "Eww. It smells like wood."

"Awfully **picky** for a war hero," I said with a **smirk.**

"Hurr**mmph!**"

"Will you guys **be quiet?**" Stump hissed.

"**Whatever,**" Emerald whispered. "It's not like we're not gonna . . ."

Just then, there was a distant sound. Beyond the trees, beyond the tall grass and flowers, came **a slight rustling.** All three of us ducked down in a sneaking position and froze. We didn't even breathe. The rustling **grew louder.** Soon it seemed as if it was almost beneath our tree. Yet I didn't see **anything.** I looked and looked through the leaves and couldn't tell what was making that noise.

148

Then it **filtered into view.** It had been invisible, and its invisibility had just worn off. Although the torches provided ample light, it was still hard to see through the leaves. Actually, it would have been hard to see even in plain view. It **blended in** with the surrounding greenery.

A creeper.

There it was, slithering toward the hole. It looked quite ordinary, but it had to be a **special** type. Perhaps this monster was another one of Herobrine's **experiments.** Or perhaps it had simply been given **Potions of Invisibility.**

The creeper looked around before **descending** into the hole. It did this in a **calm way,** as if it had done this many times before.

My friends and I **sat there.**

When we finally opened our mouths, the only things that came out were broken sentences.

Stump: "**Did you guys just see . . .**"

Emerald: "**How was it . . . I mean, it was . . .**"

Me: "**Invisible. I don't . . . um, how could it . . . so, it's actually . . .**"

149

. . . Real. The village creeper is real. Not only is it real, but it had been invisible. A scout. It had been watching us this whole time. Every day it slunk through our streets, observing. And every night it went back and reported everything it saw.

Our village was just now talking about having scouts . . . but the mobs have had them for who knows how long.

"How can it drink potions, though?" Emerald asked. "And how did it climb down the ladder? It doesn't even have arms!"

"It doesn't matter." I stood up. "This is the biggest discovery yet."

"We have to tell someone about this."

As we talked, I heard a voice call out, "What are you guys doing up there?"

Max and Breeze were not too far away, looking up at us. They had obviously come to see whether we were okay. Breeze glanced at the hole, then at the three of us standing in a tree.

She blinked in confusion.

"Did we . . . miss something?"

WEDNESDAY—SCHOOL

Last night, we told Max and Breeze what we saw. But it was so late—we weren't able to go into extreme detail. So during lunchtime at school today, we talked so much we didn't even eat.

Even though I was starving, you could have put an enchanted golden apple in front of me and I would have ignored it. Every second was spent going over the events of last night. Every little detail. We did this quietly, though. We couldn't let someone like Pebble overhear us. If he found out about the village creeper, he might get his friends and go capture it himself . . . we'd see his posters on every village block. As if I would let that happen. Tomorrow, the village is going to explode with the news: Team Runt not only found the village creeper, but captured it as well.

"There's just one problem with this idea," Max said. "How do we hold it prisoner?"

"Right," Stump said. "It can just blow itself up."

HurrMmm.

151

There were a lot of these sounds as all five of us brainstormed. Max brought up water. Creepers are filled with gunpowder, so maybe if we **drenched** it, it couldn't **explode.**

But we didn't know for sure. As far as I knew, creepers were still able to blow up even while **swimming.**

Breeze offered another solution.

"We scare it," she said. "We make it so **afraid** it won't even think about exploding."

"But how do we . . ."

Of course, **I already knew the answer.**

PROJECT DANGER KITTY II

Meet **Fluffles.** He's a **nice kitten.**

His **favorite hobbies** include:

1) eating **pufferfish;**
2) resembling **a block of wool;**
3) **scratching** the chairs in our house.

152

He also has a best friend
named **Sprinkles.**

This is what a creeper's **nightmares** look like.

Despite his name, Sprinkles is quite **large.** In fact, Sprinkles has the distinction of being the only kitten often confused for **a baby cow.** I guess a diet of bread, cookies, cakes, and pumpkin pie does that to a kitten.

As you can guess, the name of his owner is Stump.

(If I ever go on vacation, I will not let Stump take care of Jello. Will not. Will not.)

Breeze has a kitten named **Dandelion.** She named him that because of his **bright yellow fur.** Emerald and Max's kittens have **no names,** however, as they had only recently traded for them.

153

Anyway, I understand that **scratching chairs** can get boring after a while. It's time for these kittens to try out something new. Besides, when it comes to sharpening claws, what better surface is there than **a creeper's face?**

Max handed everyone **leather jerkins** that were enchanted with **Blast Protection III**—just in case. We all equipped them underneath our robes.

Project Danger Kitty II **has begun.**

We blocked off the tunnel. Then every member of Team Runt hid behind trees surrounding the hole. We waited. With kittens on leashes, we waited. We waited and waited for a very long time. Then the rustling came. The grass swayed. The creeper emerged into view. It neared the edge of the hole and whirled around. It was intelligent—it knew that something was wrong. Surely it sensed the trap. But it was too late. My heart was pounding in my chest at the thought of getting so close to such a dangerous creature. Even so, I jumped out from behind the tree, leash in hand.

"Out for a stroll?" I asked.

"Ehhgbzzt!"

It spoke in that strange language . . . but stopped once my friends stepped out.

Five villagers with five kittens (with one being very large for a kitten and quite angry looking because it hadn't had anything sugary to eat in at least five minutes).

Max stepped forward. "Slowly, guys."

155

We all converged on the green plant monster. It didn't move at all. Well, besides **a slight trembling.** *(It was shaking like a zombie villager who'd just been given a golden apple. It was absolutely, totally afraid.)*

I **pushed** Fluffles ahead one more block. My heart was beating so fast. Fluffles didn't have any **protective armor,** and his life was but a fraction of mine. If the creeper decided to **explode** . . . I'd have to dive back and yank on the leash as fast as I could . . . or my kitten **would be history.** But this had to be done. This green mass of living vegetation was why the mobs seemed to **know so much** about our village.

Even if it blew up, we could **call that a victory.** Still, it would be better if we could **capture** it, study it, learn from it . . . *(Also, if we captured it, we could walk up to the mayor with it and get medals and diamonds and have posters with us on it and be called awesome and amazing. Or just awesome. I'm not greedy!)*

Summoning the **last of my courage,** I got within one block. Breeze did **the same.** She picked up **Dandelion** and held the kitten in front of the creeper. She had that **don't-mess-with-me** look again, like when she took out those zombies during the first battle. **The creeper leaned away from her.**

She moved even closer. "Can you . . . **understand me?"**

The monster moved in a way that could be called a nod. "Y-yes. I can. Please, don't hurt me . . ." Its voice sounded like sugarcane rustling in the wind. "I don't want to blow up . . ."

I relaxed the grip on my leash. Max, Stump, and Emerald cautiously joined Breeze and me. We formed a tight ring around the monster.

Monster.
We had captured a monster.

A live one. Real. Much stronger than a baby slime.

"Put those animals away," it begged. "Please . . . the sounds they make . . ."

"We will," Emerald said, "but only after you promise to cooperate. Otherwise, you'll no longer need to imagine what a kitten's claws feel like."

It promised.
Oh, did it promise.

Surrounded by mewing kittens, it promised more than anyone had ever promised before.

Captured
Creeper!!!

STUDENTS HAVE CAPTURED THE
"EYE OF HEROBRINE"
LEGENDARY MOB
NOW IN CUSTODY

Eat that, Pebble. We captured the Eye of Herobrine. That's the name of the creeper that once stalked our streets. Brio and his men took the monster away. Probably to the same building where Brio had once taken me. There, they will figure out exactly how it manages to turn invisible. "Believe me," Brio said, "we'll make it talk."

Interrogation under way!

My parents were **in the crowd.** I could see that they were **so proud** of me. The mayor **praised** us in front of the whole village:

"Thanks to the **efforts** of these fine young villagers, we've learned of a **new threat.** In the past, the mobs have climbed over our wall and even blasted through it, but we never imagined that they might actually dig under it."

"To be honest," Kolbert said, "the Legion never thought about this, either. In the original game, the mobs never used **tools!** Their AI is **really advanced** here, I must say."

"This new game is **so cool!!**" Minsur said. "I always thought the original was a bit **too easy.** I beat it on **hardcore mode** like five or six times!"

A lot of villagers looked at them and sighed. Steve and Mike did, too. They hung out at the back of the crowd.

Anyway, the mayor was so **pleased** he decided we didn't have to go to school today or **even do chores.** And like back in the good old days—*like when I aced that building test*—other kids have been coming up to me, **congratulating me.** On top of that, Brio gave me another **payment.**

"This is for the **obsidian cube.** The mobs are still confused by it. Last night, they **covered it in dirt** to hide it from view." He handed me a

160

stack of emeralds. Then the mayor himself handed me five more.

"Those are to be split among you and your friends," the mayor said. "Good work!"

A glittering green pile. All you could hear was the sound of emeralds falling into my inventory like so much broken glass.

I'd never seen so many.
128 of them belonged to me.

Pebble, of course, was annoyed. He approached after Brio and the mayor left my presence.

"Hey, Runt."

"Hello, good sir." I patted the pocket of my robes. You could hear the emeralds shifting. "Are you here for a loan?"

"Please. You might have a lot of money, but you can't buy skill. My scores still walk all over yours."

"Someone's a sore loser," I said.

Pebble glared at me with a look that reminded me of Herobrine himself. "You're smiling now," he said, "but you won't be after that mining test. You won't be doing anything at all."

161

He shoved me.

I shoved him back. "What's your problem?"

"You're my problem," he said. "You're a noob. If you're ever tasked with defending this village, you'll be endangering us all!"

He stormed off. His words lingered in my head. Especially what he said about the mining test. That was next week. Max had mentioned something about how Pebble's father was going to rig that test.

Whatever. I'm not afraid. Lava pools, gravel traps . . . no matter what he tries, I'll avoid them all! Anyway, I'm not going to think about it right now. With no school, no homework, and no chores, it's time to relax. I'm gonna go get ice cream with my friends, and then we'll all head down to the pond. I know; I've said that before—and soon after, the village erupted into flames and smoke.

But that won't happen this time. Not today. No way. Today is mine. Mine.

I cast my line. The lure of my fishing rod went flying. You thought the mobs were gonna attack again, huh?

As did I.
As did I.

This pond is located on the south edge of the tree farm. It's more like a small lake, really. It was built to give us a place to practice swimming . . . and it serves as another source of food. Yes, we'd gone fishing.

We might be in the beginning stages of a war—a huge army of mobs will soon be knocking on our door—but even warriors in training need to rest. Every now and then.

The fishing lure bobbed slightly. I reeled in my line. A pufferfish. Surprise, surprise. I'll save it for Fluffles, I thought. After last night, it's the least I can do. Beside me, Breeze was still fumbling around with her fishing rod. She seemed a little embarrassed.

"Haven't fished much, I take it?" I asked.

163

"No, not really," she said. "Can you show me?"

"Sure. It's pretty simple, really. All you have to do is . . ."

It was strange, teaching her how to fish. She was the top student by far, and it was fishing rods that confused her. When she managed to send out her line all by herself, I'd never seen her so happy.

"Not too many lakes where you come from?" I asked.

"Actually, there were many. But since we lived so close to Herobrine's castle, our village was more focused on fighting."

"A warrior village, then."

I wasn't being serious when I said this. Yet she didn't return my grin.

"It was."

"Wait," I said. "You're saying your village actually had warriors?"

"Is it so hard to believe?"

"A little."

She looked away. "What you're experiencing now is nothing new to me. My life has always been like this. We began training at a very young age."

I didn't know what to say. She'd been a warrior even before being captured. Then whatever Herobrine did had only made her stronger.

Breeze and her father were more like **super-villagers,** then. If normal villagers were rabbits, the ones from her place were **killer bunnies.**

Pebble was right about one thing, though. **His scores are better.** To be honest, mine **haven't improved** much lately. Then again, the same can be said for everyone else. The higher our skills rise, the **harder** it becomes to improve them. For example, when my building score was low, all I had to do was place a few blocks to see an **increase.** Now it feels like I'd need to build a castle for it to jump up a single point. I think I'm hovering between **fifth** and **sixth** place. If I can just **ace** that next building test . . . Groups are allowed. Up to seven, they said. Or a student can roll solo, if he or she prefers.

"I keep having these **weird dreams,**" I said.

Breeze nodded knowingly. "Did see you **an enderman?**"

"You've been having them, too?!"

"Yes. Endermen can do a lot more than just **teleport** around. They're like **wizards,** in a way."

"Controlling dreams, huh . . ." I recalled the dream with **the strange redstone machine.**

"So that enderman is trying to help us?"

165

"I think so. My father has had those dreams, too. He thinks the enderman is working for Notch."

"Mobs? Helping Notch?"

"Not all mobs are bad, Runt."

I nodded, immediately thinking of Jello. I haven't spent much time with him lately.

On the other side of the pond, Emerald was talking to Stump and Max. They were arguing about whether the mayor was really serious about surrendering. It seems like some villagers actually think we should. I'm proud to say that none of my friends think that way. If Brio and Breeze are really so strong, maybe they can teach us how to fight. More than the humans already have, anyway.

Suddenly, Breeze's lure bobbed in the water. Her face lit up.

"Hey, Runt! I think I've caught something!"

"Reel it in!"

And she pulled in her line like Urkk himself. Her catch landed in the grass nearby. It was a book. Not only was it a book—it was a fake version of my diary. I burst out laughing. "It looks almost exactly like my diary!"

166

The more I inspected the cover, though, the more I saw the errors.

A noob had obviously crafted this forgery. The writing inside was of the same poor quality. It was so bad, in fact, I almost wondered if a zombie wrote it. Or perhaps a magma cube.

"I wonder who the author is," Breeze said.

"Pebble, most likely. Or some random noob. Who knows. If I ever find out . . . !!"

Breeze tossed the fake diary back into the pond where it belonged.

Two hours before sunset, the other three headed over to our side of the pond.

"We've been trying to come up with something to build for the test tomorrow," Max said, "and we're failing."

"It's like my mind isn't working," Emerald said. "Too much stress, you know?"

Stump mentioned a few things—TNT traps, stuff like that—but he admitted that they were all pretty stale.

"We need something fresh," he said.

"What if we think of a way to stop the mobs from tunneling under the wall?" Breeze asked.

Of course, this was something the village **desperately needed.** But I couldn't come up with anything besides **an underground obsidian wall.** We chatted for at least an hour, and nothing. At the end, Stump was strangely quiet. He was looking at something in the distance.

That was where, weeks ago, I'd **dug** up a bunch of sand to make **bottles.**

"That's it!" Stump said. "**Sand!**"

All eyes were on him. He put his hands on my shoulders.

"This time, I'm the one with the **crazy** idea."

The big day.
Building Test III.

Students had come up with all kinds of **defensive concepts.** Let's go over a few of them, shall we?

First, **Team Pebble** made a **lava trap.** There were a few people who said they just **copied Mike's house.** Still, the teachers had never seen Mike's house, and Mike wasn't around to defend himself. **So Pebble's crew made out well today.**

Team All Girls, with Emma, Mia, Sophia, and the rest, came up with something way cooler. They called it the **lava water door.** Basically, you put some **lava** over a **door** and **water** in front of it, like this: ⟶

(It can protect against the biggest explosions. The girls did a demonstration using two blocks of TNT. **What a show!***)*

169

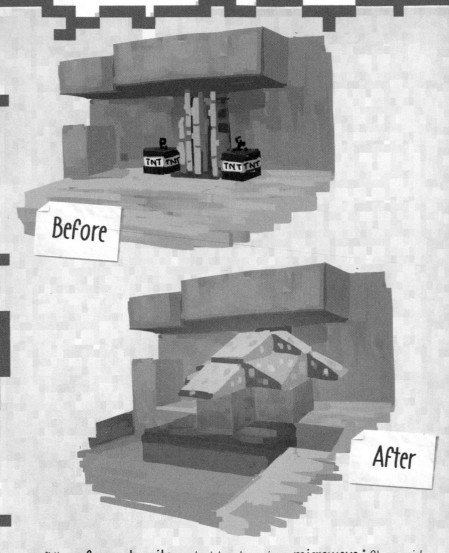

Before

After

"Like **a frozen burrito** cooked too long in a **microwave**," Steve said. The lava and water combined **to form stone.** Additional explosions could **remove** the stone, and the lava and water would continue to **make** more. A **regenerating** shield. There were a lot of **neat concepts** like this.

170

There were even a bunch of new item concepts that I will go over later.
(They're classified right now. Top secret.)

Still—and I'm not trying to brag here—nothing was as cool as what
Team Runt had come up with. You see, there's no good way to
prevent mobs from **digging under the city.** However, the village can at
least make **a system** that warns us when they do.

Allow me to explain the
Tunnel Warning System.

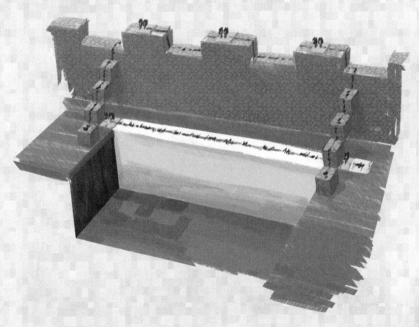

Here's how it works:

The ground in this world comes **in layers.** There's the **grass layer,** which is grass-covered dirt—that's a single block thick. Then there's the **dirt layer** underneath that. It goes down for five or so blocks, roughly. After that, it's all **stone** until you reach **bedrock** deep down.

In short, the mobs **dug a tunnel** in the dirt layer because it's way easier. Tunneling through stone takes a **very** long time. So all we'd need to do is place a wall of sand around the village in the dirt layer. Then whenever the mobs **dig through the sand,** it will collapse. This will **break** the redstone circuit on top of the sand. As a result, the redstone repeaters in that area will **no longer glow.** So the guys guarding the wall at night—**Brio's men, humans**—will at least have **some kind of warning.**

Yes, Team Runt came in first place. The teachers really **loved** this idea because we have a ton of **extra redstone** lying around.

Team All Girls came in **second,** and
Team Pebble came in **third.**

172

I have no idea what rank I am. I guess I'll find out.

Teachers and students were scattered all around. Everyone was chatting about the new inventions on display. Everyone except Breeze and me.

"Runt?"

"Yeah?"

"Are you afraid?"

"Always. If my dreams don't involve endermen, it's the mobs attacking."

"Me too. I always have nightmares about getting captured again . . . and returning to his dungeon."

"I won't let that happen," I said.

"Promise?"

"Promise."

This weekend, we're getting another break. I've decided to spend all Saturday and Sunday in the libraries with Max.

Long ago, during that second war, a lot of information was lost. Wizards' towers, the biggest libraries . . . all burned, all blown up. But if even a shred of that ancient knowledge still exists somewhere

173

in our old, dusty books, we have to find it. The stuff we build now is noob-tier compared to what the ancients once made. The rocket potion I crafted earlier is an example. Max thinks the advanced crafting table has a **five-by-five** grid instead of **three-by-three.** Crafting on a table like that would be much harder. In addition, there's an even better crafting table that has seven layers of **seven-by-seven** grids. In other words, **3-D crafting.** That's crazy. But then, what am I doing thinking about all this stuff? I don't even have **a diamond sword** yet! A diamond sword . . . It seems hard to believe, but I can actually afford one now. My friends have a sizable amount of emeralds as well.

I turned to Breeze. "Let's go find the others, huh?"

"Why? What's up?"

I reached into my inventory and gave her a **stack of emeralds.** **"We're going shopping,** that's why."

"I don't think Stump will want to join us," she said. "He keeps talking about how he wants **an obsidian sword,** just like Notch."

"I'm working on that." I winked. "This year, I plan on giving him an **early** birthday present."

174

"Speaking of Notch," she said, "it's strange that he hasn't said anything to us about the lost information. But then, maybe we're not very important . . ."

"Don't think like that." I gazed at the cloudy sky. "He's just . . . busy."

Just then, I thought I heard faint thunder coming from up there. But it wasn't stormy out. Just a layer of white clouds. Nah. It must have been my imagination.

We took off in search of our friends. I started thinking about what items I was going to buy. If I actually do buy a diamond sword, I'm gonna use all my experience points enchanting it. That thing is gonna glow so bright that if I ever meet skeletons at night, they'll start looking for trees to hide under! When Pebble sees me wielding that, can you imagine the look on his face? He took off with a scowl after he found out his team got third place.

He probably went to go work on
another fake diary.

FRIDAY—LATER

Today was one of the best days of my life. So I'm going to warn you now: I'm including a lot of details.

Details on how
I've become the—

Oops.
I almost ruined the surprise.

Emerald has **a crush** on Kolbert. At least **I think she does.** She's really secretive about it, though. I figured it out from her **reaction** to the picture I drew of him earlier. She insisted that I redraw him. In her words, to **"do him justice."** According to her, he looks way more **dashing** than my original drawing suggests. I've also been asked to point out that Kolbert doesn't actually have a beard. He just turned **fifteen.**

Wahhhhhh!
So I'd given him a beard! So what?

I think beards look funny, so I put one on him. **What's the big deal?** Also, I've apparently misspelled his name. Also, the **color** of his armor is all wrong. **Oh no!** Also, the armor itself is all wrong. He never wears a helmet. Dear **Mr. Diary,** what have I done?! The truth is I never put much time or effort into including Kolbert in my diary. Why would I? For the longest time, **the guy was a total jerk. Ordering me around.** Telling me to do this and that. I'm not your pack animal, bud. Do you see a chest **strapped** to my back?

177

All things considered, I should have made Kolbert look like a cross between an **enderman** and a **mine cart!**

Lately, however, **he's come around.** He's been **a lot nicer** to us. Courteous. Respectful. The longer he stays here, the more he involves himself with our kind. He swore to protect us, no matter what. He even saved the village from a creeper attack the other night. **All by himself.** Maybe that's why Emerald forgave him. She bought him a gift today while we were shopping at the **Clothing Castle.**

"**What?** My parents told me to buy him something," she said with a shrug. "After all, he, um, did kinda **save** us and all."

Yeah . . .

If there's one thing I learned today, it's to never let Emerald buy armor for me.

She bought him **a scarf.** Not a helmet. Not a cap or a hood. Not anything a knight might typically wear. **A black wool scarf.** I told her that Kolbert would probably go diving in the Nether before putting that thing on. Puddles, **the shopkeeper,** thought otherwise.

"But it's the same color as his armor," she said. "Don't worry, **sugar block. He'll love it!**"

178

Yes, Puddles is a she, not a he. She has a deep voice for a woman and wears a **witch-style hat** so low that you can't really see her face.

I need to start paying more attention.

"He'll like it," Emerald said. "After all, this scarf is enchanted with **Protection III**."

Stump spit out bits of pumpkin pie. "**Protection III?!** How much did you spend on that?"

"**Two stacks.**"

Two stacks of emeralds. **Sure,** that sounds about right. That's about what **a diamond goes for** these days. To our shocked expressions, she rolled her eyes.

"Those came out of my father's inventory. Not mine. He says we need to **strengthen our alliance** with the humans."

When she said that, our eyes grew even **wider.** Puddles made **a slight gasp.** She didn't know much about the humans and thought their **taste in fashion was terrible.**

"Side with them? Now, why would we do that?"

AN ALLIANCE?

179

It's not **unthinkable.** We **need** them and they **need** us. But first, the humans will have to come to terms with their issues. Right now, there are **a lot** of humans in our village. New ones wander in every day. **Strangely enough,** they've become divided into **two factions,** each with entirely **different beliefs.** One group believes that this world isn't real. They're known as **the Seekers—seekers of the truth.** If you ask them, this is all some kind of elaborate **virtual reality show.** Alternatively, it's the result of some accident involving their Earth **technology.** That group throws around many **theories,** attempting to explain this world in human terms. In their way of thinking, it doesn't matter how they treat us, because **NPCs don't have real feelings.** To them, even if we display **emotions,** that's the result of programming, **scripting, AI**—stuff I don't understand.

The other group **disagrees.** They call themselves **the Believers.** They believe in the **impossible:** that the game has somehow **come to life.** At the very least, they've given up trying to understand and have come to accept this world for what it is. The two groups often have heated discussions over this. They discuss it more than they do **pizza,** which is saying something. Their biggest quarrel occurred when **Kolbert,** their leader, suddenly changed his mind. He's a **Believer** now.

"These people are real," he said the other day. "As such, they should be treated accordingly."

I only hope he can sway some more humans to his side . . . Call me picky, but I like it better when they don't treat us like slaves.

Kolbert talks about that stuff in his diary. I read most of the entries. I even copied one section down. It's from a few days ago, when Emerald tried speaking to him.

That villager girl talked to me again. It was eerie. Seeing her sent chills down my spine. There was emotion in her voice. Warmth in her smile. A soul behind her eyes. I had once assumed that these people were NPCs. But right then, the truth became so clear. Standing before me, a girl who was once just polygons was now real live flesh and blood. Although I couldn't understand how this had happened . . . I understood that it had happened.

A world made of cubes—once so many countless pixels—had inexplicably sprung to life.

Hurmmm. I want to get a full copy of his diary now. By the way, we ran into him after we left the Clothing Castle. Emerald gave him the scarf—and crazily enough, he actually liked it.

181

DESPITE WHAT RUNT
SAID, I'M NOT A
<u>WIMP</u>.

I WEAR THIS
SCARF
BECAUSE IT
GREATLY
STRENGTHENS MY
DEFENSE.

IT IS A MERE
COINCIDENCE THAT
IT ALSO HIGHLIGHTS
MY PERFECT HAIRSTYLE.

A lot of kids at school joke about how he acts like a **wuss** sometimes. A little girly. Come Monday, after they spot him walking around with that thing on, that's all we're gonna hear.

Not every human is like Kolbert, **though.** Many are still **rude** to us, making comments. My friends and I passed some of them on the street.

"What are they wearing?! **Ninja outfits?!**"

"**Forget the robes!** It's still strange to see villagers wielding swords!"

"**Hey!** That's the kid who's always running around being weird! What's his name again? **Grunt?**"

"You mean they actually **have names?**"

"Let's go see what they have to trade."

Villagers wielding swords?!
Villagers having names and being weird?!

Those things just aren't supposed to happen, I guess. We're supposed to just walk around randomly, make strange noises, and sometimes . . . if we're feeling **adventurous** . . . **plant** new vegetables.

Big adventures
in a little village:
Part I

Will Grunt manage
to plant the carrot?!?

Oh no, be careful—
you're planting it next to the potatoes!!!

184

The humans continued talking as if we weren't even there.

"I don't want to trade with them. They're creepy. Besides, it's not like they have macaroni or something."

"Oh, man. Macaroni. I'd pay fifty emeralds for a single bowl!"

"Or some spaghetti . . ."

"With some garlic bread . . ."

"Topped with sprinkle cheese . . ."

The last two lines were said by human boys whose eyes started watering.

Hurggg!!

Stop crying already and eat some pumpkin pie, you noobs!!!

Stump gave the humans a tired look. "Maybe I should figure out how to craft a large pepperoni," he said in a low tone.

"If you did," Breeze said, "villagers everywhere would rejoice. You'd probably get voted in as the new mayor."

Yeah, don't even get them started on pizza. They have heated arguments over it. "Supreme" this. "Stuffed crust" that. "Ham and pineapple all the way."

Suddenly, I had a great idea. Maybe I could try to make a few emeralds off their **pizza craze.** You see, this world already has pizza. **Kind of.** In a way. So I'll sell it to them and **profit!** Here's a poster I'm thinking about using for **my future pizza shop:**

CRISPY
PUMPKIN
PIZZA

WITH SAUCE AND TOPPINGS
MADE FROM
MASHED PUMPKIN

Pumpkin pizza?!
How crazy is that?!
You think you're hardcore with pineapple on your pizza?!
I don't even know what pineapple is, but honestly, you're not a **REAL** pizza fan until you've tried a pizza topped with glorious, glorious pumpkin!! *(Diamond armor, here I come!!)*

186

The five of us eventually arrived at **Leaf's shop.** In case you forgot, he's **the cranky old blacksmith** I scammed a long time ago.

Yeah. That guy. I can't say **why** we chose to visit him. Maybe we were too busy thinking about **trading** for more cool stuff. Come on, how could anyone not get excited at the thought of trading for **cool stuff?!** Max likes trading for cool stuff. Stump likes trading for cool stuff. Drill, the mayor, this one human named **Sami—**

everyone likes trading for cool stuff!

I classify **cookies** as cool stuff, but when I get one, I immediately eat it and have to trade for another all over again.

Also, Breeze has **never traded** for cool stuff before because she used to live in a village where she couldn't trade for cool stuff. Still, when I asked her if she wanted to trade for cool stuff, her face totally **lit up** like a firework rocket enhanced with a fire charge. Even cows would like trading for cool stuff, probably, except they don't have **hands** with which to hold emeralds.

Unfortunately, for a cow, "cool stuff" just means "grass."

If cows could trade, grass farming would be a thing—and tools with Silk Touch would be even more valuable.

So we had **a plan,** then. We still had **a bunch** of emeralds and wanted to keep shopping. There was **one problem.** We were about to buy new weapons. We had to do it in a cool way. We had to do it like warriors, **you know?** In my opinion, *real* warriors would probably do the following:

1) Go into a **blacksmith's** shop.

2) Slam the **emeralds** onto the table.

3) Ask to buy **weapons** that would make an obsidian golem cry.

188

4) Give the blacksmith **a mean look.** I mean, **mean.** The kind of look that says, *"Don't mess with me. **I'm tough.*** *In fact, I'm* **SO tough** *I have an item called Noob-On-A-Stick which allows me to ride ender dragons as if they were giant winged pigs."*

Yeah, that's what
real warriors would do.

So we did. Of course, considering what happened last time, Leaf just **laughed.**

"You call those **emeralds,** kids? I know yer **tricks.**
Just a bunch of dyed green glass."

He actually **bit into** one just to see whether it was real. *(I'm not sure why his biting an emerald would prove anything though, because he doesn't even have teeth.)*

When he realized our emeralds were—**unbelievably-real emeralds,** his face lit up like a firework—rocket explosion enhanced not by a fire charge but a creeper head instead—**which is just crazy.** Don't try to imagine that, okay?! **I'm still trying to forget.**

189

So anyway, at least now we had Leaf's attention. "Make an obsidian golem cry, huh?" he said. He pointed at an iron pickaxe. "What about that? I bet that would do the job."

We gave him blank looks.

"You need diamonds to mine obsidian," Breeze said calmly.

"Oh. Of course, of course. I was just, um, testing you. No noobs allowed in my shop, see."

Awkward silence.
More blank stares.

The blacksmith glanced around his shop.

"How about this?" he asked, holding up an iron sword.

The sword wasn't enchanted and had low durability on top of that.

(Actually, it looked like it was only a few swings away from breaking.)

He looked at our still-blank faces and shrugged. "Well, it will definitely make a ghast cry. Guaranteed! Or yer emeralds back."

"Dude," Stump said, "are you joking? A pink tulip would make a ghast cry!"

190

Max sighed. "Imagine a sword that was so bad it actually healed whatever it struck. It would still make a ghast cry."

"Hurmpph!" Emerald whirled around. "That piece of junk would make me cry . . . if I traded for it."

Breeze just shook her head and left.

Everyone else was quick to follow her out the door, but I took one last glance around at Leaf's items. Something caught my eye. It was round and slightly shiny, bluish-green in color. An ender pearl. They're quite rare around here. It was only five emeralds, too. I'd been wanting to buy Breeze a gift anyway and thought she might like to have one.

Wow.

Breeze used to annoy me,
and now I'm buying her stuff?!
What's going on here?!

Without another word, I joined my friends in search of another place to spend our hard-earned gemstones.

191

As we made our way to another blacksmith, there was a distant shout. Far away, some humans were standing on the wall. Christina and Sami were among them—two humans I actually like. They were shouting, although I couldn't hear what they were saying from this distance. Also, I couldn't see what they were looking at. The wall was totally blocking my view. It didn't matter. If there's one thing I've learned from growing up in my village, it's that shouting is bad. Is there any kind of shout around here that isn't followed by a wave of zombies, people running in terror, explosions, and/or burning houses? Usually, no.

So we ran to the east wall. Gone were my dreams of spending some serious gemstones. Gone were my dreams of enchanted boots, a new sword, and more gifts for my friends. As we got closer to the wall, the only thing filling my head was what the terrified humans kept screaming.

"Slimes!"

"There're SO many!"

"Why don't we surrender already?!"

So the village was under attack.

192

It was going to be **a totally normal weekend,** then. I mean, this village can't possibly have a weekend without a random mob attack! It's **tradition** around here! Apparently, the mobs in **Mob City** have classes in Mob School only during the weekdays, and during Mob Weekend, **it's something like this:**

Your homework for the weekend . . . **terrorize the village.**

The enderman hung his head. It was supposed to rain all weekend.

193

Still, from what the humans were saying, it was just **some slimes out there.**

Slimes usually aren't **a very big deal.** It's not like they can wield pickaxes, unless Herobrine found a way to give them **arms.**

They were probably going to **creeperbomb** us. Have the humans never seen a creeperbomb before? There's a lot of **commotion** after one, sure. Baby villagers **crying.** Young girls **screaming.** Tiny slimes **bouncing everywhere.** But these days, it's not exactly what we could consider **an emergency.** The little slimes don't deal any damage—they're just really annoying. And we've come to realize that a creeperbomb is an excellent source of slimeballs. If anything, we're now **thankful** for such attacks, because slimeballs **can be used to craft cool stuff.**

And let me tell you **right now**—to a villager, there's only one thing better than cool stuff, and that's free cool stuff. So I hadn't even climbed up the ladder yet to see what all the fuss was about. **I didn't have to.** My plan was I'd just wait for the green cubes to come **raining down,** play **Whack-a-Slime,** and profit.

194

(I only wished they could have attacked after I'd bought a new sword so that I could test it out on them right away. Those mobs are so inconsiderate!)

I told my friends about the plan. Max, Stump, and Emerald thought it was a great idea. Breeze, however, made no comment. Instead, she climbed up the ladder. (I'm guessing that was her way of saying my plan stunk worse than zombie breath.) What is she doing?! I thought. The slimes will rain down in the city, not on the wall! The streets will be filled with slimeballs! We have to be the first ones to collect them! Slimeballs sell for, like, one emerald each! Emeralds might as well be falling from the sky!

Hurmmmph.

I went up the wooden rungs after her. By the time I reached the top, everyone had stopped shouting. A bunch of humans and a few villagers were just staring at the forest without a word. I quickly understood why. A huge row of slimes stood out there, in front of their forest. Now, everyone knows that slimes hop around constantly. They never stop bouncing. Not these, though. No, they didn't move at all.

195

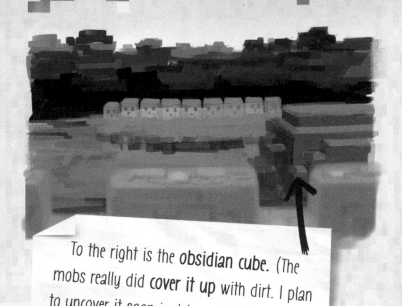

To the right is the **obsidian cube.** (The mobs really did **cover it up** with dirt. I plan to uncover it soon just to **mess with them.**)

It was **unsettling** to say the least. A row of slimes, just sitting there, **motionless.** It was like **watching** a skeleton hug a wolf—

totally unnatural.

I really hope **Jello** doesn't get as fat as these guys. **He's totally going on a diet.**

196

After Emerald joined us up top, she made a slight gasp.

"Well, this is new."

Max slowly stepped toward the edge of the wall. "They must be . . . practicing."

"Practicing? Practicing what?"

"Formations, I think."

I suddenly had a horrible idea. Maybe our village is just like a practice dummy to the mobs. Maybe they've been studying us. Learning from us. Using us to improve their techniques.

Which means . . . when they finally destroy us, they'll be experienced enough to handle the real villages to the west. Could it be? Is that all we are to them? A training ground?

A tutorial?

A hands-on test called

How to Properly Destroy Walled Villages?

Before long, the slimes began advancing.

That Herobrine . . . he sure has those mobs trained.

They all hopped **at the same time.** They looked like a bouncing wall of goo. Naturally, this caused **a lot of commotion.** Perhaps one-third of the village had gathered on the wall. **A small army** of villagers and humans—mixed together, bows ready, faces grim— **studying the approaching enemy.**

"What are they doing?"

"Why are they all lined up like that?"

"Are they about to have a race or something?"

Soon, everyone realized the purpose of **today's attack.** Slimes are somewhat **transparent.** You can see through them. As they inched closer, I started to make out more mobs **behind them.**

You could also see their feet whenever the slimes jumped up. **Nice try, mobs.** You are NOT that sneaky.

HIHIHIHI

198

It was a solid strategy, though.
After today, we're calling it the slime wall.
The slimes were acting as shields to protect the creepers.

They were testing whether slimes would be enough to bring creepers close to the wall. If the troops made a large hole, it would take too long to repair. A huge army of zombies could then pour in. It would take a huge amount of arrows just to break through those meat shields.

Their little plan had one major flaw, of course:

Me and the small mountain of arrows that I now haul around at all times.

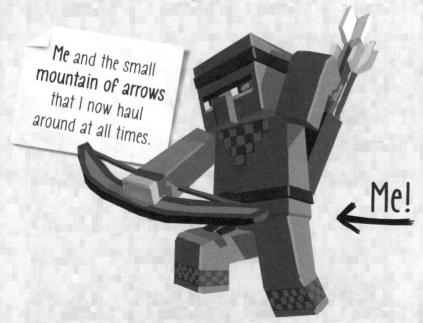

← Me!

199

Well, not just me. There were a lot of us. These days, everyone carries two stacks of arrows in his or her inventory. At least two stacks. My grandfather carries around three. And TNT. And a lava bucket. And a water bucket, because why not?

Did I ever mention that my grandfather doesn't like mobs? Maybe it just runs in the family. Some zombies trashed his flowerpots a long time ago. He's sworn vengeance ever since. I haven't talked to him much since I started school, but he taught me a lot.

Actually. I didn't speak much at all before I started school. Maybe it's a family thing.

Anyway, we had **enough arrows** to turn every last slime out there into **a huge supply of leashes,** slime blocks, and sticky pistons.

Then, once the slimes fell, **the creepers** could be easily picked off before they could cause any real damage. Simple, **right?**

There's **two steps** in the plan:

1. THE MOBS APPROACH ON FOOT.

2.

WE SHOOT ARROWS FROM ABOVE.

Top secret villager tactics, I know.

It's not exactly redstone science. Until today, though, that was our plan for pretty much **any mob attack.** Almost any mob-related problem can be solved with a **ridiculous amount of arrows.** Almost **any.** But today, that strategy didn't work out so well . . .

Breeze was standing on the very edge of the wall, next to Brio. **At her father's command,** she pulled back her bowstring all the way. (The only other student strong enough to do that is Pebble.)

Then there was **a loud twang.** Her arrow made the sharpest sound as it cut through the air. And even though the slimes were still some ways away, I heard a **wet slap** as the projectile **sank** into one of them.

202

Strangely,

nothing happened.

The slime quivered slightly, but that was it. It was as if the slime hadn't taken any damage at all. Beside her, Pebble drew **Sir Mobspanker II, his enchanted bow.** "Let me **show you** how to shoot," he said to Breeze. "Then you can go back to your **wool crafting.**"

Calm as always, she only smirked and said in a cold way, "Weren't you the one asking me for **archery lessons** the other day?"

There were a few gasps. Behind him, Mia and Emma **laughed.** Also, Priyanka, Nadia, Kaylee, Ben, Bekah . . . yeah. **A lot of kids laughed.**

Pebble's cheeks turned **red.** "Like I need archery lessons from a nooblord like—"

"Enough!" Brio shouted.

All laughter **ceased immediately.** Then Pebble **scowled** and turned back to the slimes. Like Breeze, he unleashed an arrow that had enough force to one-shot a zombie **in leather.**

No effect.

Face reflecting both anger and confusion, the "war hero" sent out another arrow. Again, it was as if the slime had been struck by a snowball, not an arrow driven with Punch I. Immune. It was like they were somehow immune to arrows. If watching the motionless slimes earlier was like seeing a skeleton hugging a wolf, well . . . this was like a skeleton and a wolf being bred to create something I don't even want to imagine. It was the craziest thing we'd seen yet.

There were a few seconds of total silence. Then everyone exploded into blind panic all at once.

"What is this?!"

"Their arrows had no effect?!"

"Pebble and Breeze are the very best! How is this even possible?!"

The mayor looked super scared, like a noob who'd built a small base but forgot to light one small section, and a creeper spawned there, and the base had a hole in the roof, so lightning struck the creeper, turning it into a charged creeper, which blew up the noob's entire . . . base.

Um. Never mind.
The mayor looked really scared.

"Are you two using **those things** correctly?!" he asked, meaning their bows.

Yeah. **Sounds about right.** A wall of slimes, backed by creepers, was slowly crawling toward Villagetown, and everyone around me was freaking out. **No, not everyone.** Breeze and Pebble had both fired shots, so I thought it'd be a good idea if **I did, too.** With **sudden anger,** I almost pulled my bowstring back all the way. **Almost.** That arrow went soaring. **There was so much power behind it.**

So much.

Huge. Huge power.

Whatever, dude. I was just trying to see if it'd flinch. Scare tactics, **bro.** Scare tactics. Get on my level.

Max **nudged me.**

"I think those slimes are **enhanced** somehow. Remember what I told you about **rune chambers?**"

"You mean they're enchanted?"

"Something like that."

I recalled what little Max had told me about the so-called rune chambers. They're extremely advanced—about ten times harder to construct than an enchanting table with a full set of bookshelves.

Today, everything changed.
Today, we finally realized
just what we were up against.

Everything we villagers had learned in school . . . everything the humans had learned in the computer game . . . all that was just the basics. Baby mode.

At the basic level, you know that a slime is difficult to drop because it splits into smaller slimes. Past that, we've learned that mobs work together—zombies and slimes stand in front of more important mobs to protect them, for example. But today, things were taken to a whole new level and training for the real stuff began. Up on that wall, we were noobs all over again. A few kids around me looked at the slime formation with actual tears in their eyes.

206

It was Drill who pulled us to our senses.

"They may be able to protect against our arrows, but **anti-sword protection** does not exist!!!" Drill shouted.

Look at Stump staring at Drill's diamond sword. We can only dream . . .

He was right. We had to go **down there.** We had to go down there and show those mobs **a few good swords.** No longer could we stand upon a wall and **fire a small forest's worth of projectiles** until nothing moved. We had to climb down those ladders, open that gate, and come pouring out, screaming, ready to defend our biome village. There were about twenty slimes out there, though . . . big slimes, too. Just over two and a half blocks in size.

I'd heard stories about how large slimes can swallow a rabbit, a chicken, or even a block of dirt whole. Well, I'm not that small, but then . . . I'm not that big, either!!

Suddenly, my legs felt too heavy to move. Suddenly, it was like I'd forgotten how to climb down ladders. I wasn't scared, though. I was probably under the effects of some kind of magic. Yeah.

It's the strangest thing, too. Everyone else around me was suffering from the same mysterious spell. Brio, of course, helped Drill in removing this debuff.

"This is it," he said. "This is the day we drive back the enemy. The day we've all been waiting for."

"Yeah," Emerald muttered to Breeze. "I've been waiting for today . . . and would be happy to continue waiting for at least five thousand years. Possibly six. I'm patient."

208

The mayor **joined** Brio and Drill
with his own little speech.

"If we fail today . . . we will all **become slaves.**"

You'll salute creepers.

You'll lick zombie boots.

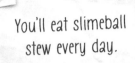

You'll eat slimeball stew every day.

Slimeballs are used in lots of their recipes. They raise them like cows or pigs.

"Now they're telling us kids' stories to make us scared? There's no such thing as slimeball stew."

No, they're telling the truth.

"My dad knew the recipe. Right up there with slimeball stew is herb stew. **Nothing like ice cream.** Ice cream with cookie pieces . . . and bits of cake."

Protect!!! The village!!!
AHHHHHHHHHGGGGG!!!

Why is this guy still fighting with a wooden sword?!

You can't really see our mouths because of our ninja masks, but believe me, we were screaming.

EPIC BATTLE. We charged out of that gate. Angry. Scared. Desperate. *(Some of us were also kind of hungry.)* No one wanted to imagine a future in which mobs ruled. No one wanted to imagine a day when eating things like slimeball stew was totally okay, even fashionable. Drill surged past me, uttering the loudest battle cry, and repeated what he said earlier about how our swords would tear through them.

211

Boy, was he wrong. After those first few swings, we realized that our swords were doing almost no damage. It was like trying to drop an ender dragon with your bare hands—possible, sure, and brag-worthy to your friends, okay, but very, very time-consuming.

"It's their armor," Max said. He took another swing. "It's the only explanation for this."

That was certainly possible. If the slimes were resistant to both arrows and melee weapons, an increase in armor was most likely the reason.

"Hurmm. Are they under some kind of potion effect? Stoneskin?"

I remembered that battle with the zombies. Their armor was so high that my sword more or less bounced off them. It was just like this. Still, even large slimes don't deal that much damage. All we had to do was stay away from the hungry-looking ones.

(For anyone who says slimes don't eat things, just come to my world. After one looks at you like you're a giant cookie with legs, you will cry. CRY.)

It would have taken time, but we could have chipped away at their life until they eventually dropped. Together, Breeze and Pebble had already removed half of a slime's health bar.

We were making progress!

By the way, you might be thinking to yourself, *"If they wanted to reach the creepers, why didn't they just run around the slimes?"*

I might go down in battle someday, but not like that.

Herobrine must have **known** that we'd try this. So he told the mobs to bring backup . . . **just in case.** Behind trees, **hidden in shadow,** they'd been waiting there the whole time. As soon as we tried moving around the slimes, they charged out. **There were so many of them.**

That Herobrine . . .
what a guy.

I hate to say this, **but he really is a genius,** you know?

He rounded up these mobs, **trained** them, and buffed them somehow. **These mobs were so noob before, you know?!** Back when I was a **little kid,** you could confuse a zombie with a dirt block. **A dirt block!**

Then they start planting trees, **spying** on us, chugging down ten potions before battle . . . **now this?!**

At that point, I understood that our strength **didn't matter at all.** Brute force wasn't the answer here. No. **We needed something else.**

A flaw. A weakness.
A hole in their defenses.

Something that Herobrine had never imagined.

We needed to think. Unfortunately, the only thing anyone was thinking of right then was survival.

"Back inside!!" Drill shouted. "Retreat!! Retreat, you bedrock jockeys!! You're moving like mine carts off rails!!"

"The Legion never retreats!!" Kolbert stepped forward, surveying the approaching swarm. "Actually, in this case, I think we can make an exception."

Within seconds, everyone was running.
Everyone.

If a Nether portal had been around, some of us probably would have jumped in just to escape; we were that terrified.

I'll be completely up-front here: I also ran. Yes, that's right. Runt, the kid who dreams of someday becoming Overlord Runt, ran away.

But I stopped. For some strange reason, I just stopped running and watched everyone go. The mayor's words echoed in my head. If we are defeated today, we will all become slaves.

What are we doing? I thought. *We can't give up so easily. So we can't deal with the slimes, but we can still* **take out the creepers,** *right? With the creepers gone, those slimes won't matter at all. Of course.*

Still, I was alone. No one even looked back. No one had any second thoughts. I can't blame them. They were just **following Drill's orders.** Besides, we hadn't trained for this kind of situation. **We were totally disorganized.**

Even as the mobs **approached,** I stared at the wall. Behind me, I heard the **slimes crawling, the zombies breathing . . .**

Suddenly, I pictured all the kids who lived in my village. **Every last one.** Some I barely knew. Regardless, I knew at least one thing about each of them.

They all had **dreams.**

Hopes. Secret little wishes.

Just like me.

A kid named Tucker dreamed of having **a rabbit farm.**

A somewhat shy girl named Tessa dreamed of constructing a flying **machine.**

There must have been over **one hundred** of them, each with their own dream. Thrasher, who hoped to **improve the combat cave.** Olivine, Shelby, and Anna, who wanted to **become expert horse riders.** Enderstorm, whose goal in life was someday **mapping the End.** There was even a human named **Bobbyzilla** who hoped to **start a human city near us.** One after another, they flashed across my mind, clear, like **paintings** on a wall. If those mobs reached our village, their dreams and ideas would never turn into reality. Drago's lavaspring trap. Flamewolf's note block music machine. Skyler's restaurant featuring legendary, hard-to-craft food.

All that would be gone.
I turned around for them.

They were **the reason** I reached into my inventory. After remembering all of them, **I had come up with an answer.** For this, both sword and bow went into the extra-dimensional space of my inventory.

My bow was too bulky. I needed something **easier to handle.**

My iron sword was too heavy. I needed to replace it with **something lighter.**

Watch out, mobs! Welcome to the crash course, "**How to Destoy a Village.**" You'd better sit down, because I have some bad news. **I will be your teacher today.**

219

. . . and you all get a **zero !!!**

I started **running** at the slime wall. As I neared it, **I threw that ender pearl high into the air.** I'd never thrown one before and had no idea just **how far up it would go.**

It felt like
forever.

I reached the slimes while the pearl was still **high in the air.** They looked at me; I looked at them. Then I started running back to the village.

At last, like an arrow that had been shot almost straight up, the ender pearl came **crashing down.**
Behind them. And suddenly, **I was behind them,** too.

The ender pearl. 9 out of 10 ninjas recommend that you carry at least 3 at all times, whatever happens.

The ninja who doesn't agree is obviously an undercover enderman.

The slimes and creepers were **totally confused.** I had been running away from them, **and then I'd vanished.** Surely I had teleported in the direction I was running, **right?** They had no idea that I was close, just three blocks behind them. The zombies spotted me, though, since they were facing me, and swarmed in my direction.

That was right where I wanted them. Everything was falling exactly into place. You see, I'd learned in Mob Defense that **flint and steel** could cause creepers to begin their detonation sequence. **It takes only a single hit**—against them, flint and steel might as well be **an obsidian sword** with **Bane of Plants XXVIII.** Of course, they still blow up, which is usually an undesired effect.

In this situation, though, well . . . that was more like <u>a bonus.</u>

Thank you, Professor Snark. (He's the new Mob Defense teacher. Former owner of that tavern the mobs blew up. Yeah. He wants revenge.)

I sprinted away just as the **first blast** went off. Unable to **react in time, the zombies were obliterated.** The large slimes broke down into **medium ones.** They were trapped in the **trench the blasts had created.** The skeletons retreated back into the woods. I'm not sure why. **They could have finished me off.** There must have been a reason . . .

I took a step back. My ears were **ringing.** My heart was **pounding.** Worse, my vision was **flashing red.** I was in so much pain. I hadn't moved entirely out of the blast radius, **so I'd taken a lot of damage.**

Before that, I'd suffered falling damage from **the ender pearl.** I'd forgotten all about that. **I was in a state of shock.** Despite this, my mind was still functioning: **There were three things left to do.**

1) Eat a **cookie.**

2) Eat **another cookie.**

3) Eat **another cookie.**

Crumbs **flying,** my hunger bar was finally topped off. **My health bar** slowly began to fill back up. I know. **Facepalm.** Not only had I forgotten about the ender pearl's damage, but I hadn't thought to **eat** before the battle. Go ahead, laugh at me. I'm not a noob, however. I'm only slightly noob—technically not a full one. No, scratch that. I'm just not Steve level yet, okay?

Life no longer in the red, I gazed at the smoking chasm. The slimes tried hopping out, but there was no place to climb up.

No one messes with Villagetown on my watch, I thought. No one.

Well, except ender cave spiders, I mean. If those things start attacking us, I'm becoming a cow farmer and/or milk bucket salesman. My shop will also be in the sky. In a rain cloud.

For a second there, I felt so cool. Blown-up zombies strewn all around. A smoking crater full of defeated slimes. The wind caught the smoke just then, making it drift across me. All I needed was the steely gaze of a warrior.

Oh, and a cool one-liner.

"Guess you guys didn't have Blast Protection."

(Wait a second. Doesn't armor protect against explosions?)

224

I walked over to the **edge of the pit.** A **countless** number of slimes **trembled helplessly.** Then I retrieved the lava bucket from my inventory. Due to the **incredible heat,** it was uncomfortable to hold for any length of time. A **weird** feeling came over me. It felt like I was beginning to change in some way. Yet I wasn't sure if that **change** was entirely . . . good. **The bucket trembled in my hands.** No, I wouldn't be pouring lava on those slimes. If a zombie comes charging at me, I'll give it arrows until it resembles **a guardian fish,** but this—**not for anything.**

What was my problem?
Was I getting _soft_ or something?

Pebble would have done it **without a second thought,** like he was **watering** crops. I really can't explain what came over me. **It just felt wrong somehow.** Even if they were mobs. Or maybe I just thought of Jello. **Who knows?**

As the smoke **cleared,** I noticed some people standing on the wall. They were waving, shouting, pointing. They were cheering for me. **Or so I thought.**

Then I heard a crunching sound behind me . . . *tch, tch, tch* . . .

BOSS BATTLE?!

One of the things we've been learning in Mob Defense is how to identify a monster by the sound of its footsteps. Well, from behind me came the sound of iron boots across grass.

I was certain. I whirled around.
Oh.
Okay.
Not iron.
Gold, enchanted to the brim.

A zombie in a full suit, with a sword to match. So shiny. Apparently, that's the fashion over there in Mob City.

He was probably their commander. It wasn't fair. I was way too tired for a boss fight. Judging by the look on his face, I doubted he'd wait around for my health bar to refill. Not even if I said "pretty please with a charged creeper head on top." After he got within stinky-breath distance, the zombie spoke:

226

At night, when he's not harassing villagers, **Angryface McSparklebutt** stands on Mob City's tallest tower so lost mobs can find their way home.

"Ten creepers. **Not bad.** I hope that was worth **the pain** you're about to experience."

With **impossible speed,** the zombie threw a potion using his left hand. It happened so fast. In my tired state, there was **no way** I could have avoided it.

It struck me right in the chest. The glass bottle shattered against my body. Liquid splashed out and evaporated into a cloud of **grayish-blue swirls.** Surprisingly, there was no pain. **I took a step back.** It was the slowest step I'd ever taken. I might as well have been walking underwater. On top of that, my whole body felt weighed down, like I was wearing **armor made of anvils** or something.

227

The truth immediately became clear. The zombie had hurled a

Slowness Potion. It must have had some kind of **enhanced** effect,

too. Normally, that kind of **potion reduces your speed** to that of a

crawl. This, however, was more like moving through cobwebs over soul

sand over ice. Slower than that, even.

To quote Drill,
"like a mine cart off the rails."
Hurggg.

Who would have expected a zombie to throw **a splash potion?**

I opened my mouth to shout for help, then closed it. It'd only make

me look like a **wuss.** It was pointless anyway. No doubt everyone was

already charging back here. **As if that would help.** By the time they

arrived, they'd find only a pile of items on the ground . . .

If he doesn't loot me first, I thought. And he probably will, if I know

funky-looking zombies.

Huh?
What's that?

Something was moving slightly in the corner of my eye. It was past the zombie, past the dirt-covered obsidian cube. Yes, hiding behind the dirt mound was a familiar thin black form . . .

Figures.
I turned my back to the zombie.
Well, at least I can relax now.

A gentle wind drifted through the plains. In addition, the flowers around here were quite lovely. I closed my eyes and took in their fragrance. Thankfully, the zombie was upwind.

"Turn around and face me," the mob said from behind. "You have no chance of running."

"Running . . ." I caught the flowery scent once more. "No, I'm afraid you're the one who should be doing that."

"Oh?" Deep laughter erupted at my back. "And why is that?"

"You'll find out soon enough."

To the casual observer, I should have been afraid. At the very least, I shouldn't have turned my back on him. This zombie was quite powerful, deserving of the title "mini boss."

Alone, the only way I could have defeated him was through superior footwork, which, given this current debuff, was **impossible.** Yet it no longer mattered. I knew who was out here. I'd caught her movements. After today, only one thing is for certain. No matter where I go or how much danger I'm in . . . **she will always be there.**

And since I had **promised to protect her . . .**

She made me
a promise
in return . . .

It was something she would **never say** in words.

But she had **always been there for me.**

SATURDAY—MORNING

Yesterday, **Breeze gave me a hug.** This morning, we actually **held hands.** Um, technically, I guess. It's really not what you're thinking.

I'm hanging this in my bedroom—and some day, I'll craft a **gold frame.**

We had a **huge** celebration.

The mayor joined us up there, along with Brio, Drill, and many other teachers. **Rose petals** were flying everywhere.

233

"Herobrine's forces are constantly **improving,**" the mayor said, "and yesterday, their attack caught us all **off guard.** Yet two brave young villagers stood up to them. **Aspiring warriors everywhere should take notes.**"

Unbelievable, right?

You never thought you'd see the day, huh, Mr. Diary?

As of today,
Breeze and I are officially war heroes.

We received **special cloaks,** too. Wanna know what's **super amazing** about that? Our cloaks are actually **better** than the ones Pebble and Emerald have.

THE VICTORY
CLOAK
SUREFOOTED II
SAFEGUARD I

Free cool stuff. Free cool stuff. Free cool . . . **control yourself,** Runt. **Control yourself.**

The cloak comes with not one but two really amazing enchantments. Surefooted is for knockback resistance. The usefulness of that goes without saying.

As for Safeguard . . . if I have very low life, a protective effect will kick in. It only can do this once per full moon, but it's still amazing.

Kolbert was also praised for his defense of the village the other night. I wasn't surprised to hear Pebble's friends making jokes about his new scarf. Notice how I said, "Pebble's friends," not "Pebble and his friends." Pebble didn't say anything. He was like that since the start of the celebration. He took off with Rock when the speeches were over and it was time to eat. He seemed angry, although I could tell he was trying to hide it. Who cares. No need to dwell on someone like him. Good food was everywhere, and everyone else was so happy.

It was the biggest party
we'd ever had.

Even Breeze smiled. A rare moment. Once more, she ran her fingers across her new cloak. She's never really had a good item before. Now I feel guilty for using that ender pearl . . .

I was thinking about what to buy as a replacement gift when Drill came up to me.

"Good work out there, Runt. Keep it up. Some day you might be calling me endermite."

He shook my hand. Thankfully I was still wearing my hood because my cheeks must have been as red as a redstone block. The combat teacher raised a bottle of melon juice. A flavored drink. The village's very first. Something Tails and Maya had come up with.

"I don't know if you'll manage to become a captain, though." He took a glug. "Tough competition this year. Pebble sure has it out for you."

My mind totally froze.

Captain?!

Why had I never heard
anything about this?!

236

At my obvious confusion, Drill's smile **faded.** "Never mind," he said.

He took off in a hurry after that, before I could ask any questions. Breeze turned to me as Drill vanished into the crowd. "Why do I get the **feeling** the mayor's going to make a big announcement today?" she asked.

Indeed. Even before Drill had come over, I'd sensed something **different** about the teachers today. You could see it in their expressions. Hear it in their laughter as they chatted together in small groups. **Nervousness.** Yesterday was the biggest **victory** our village has seen. Yet, at the same time, the monsters surprised us, as they always have . . . I thought about this for a moment, but yeah—you know how my mind **wanders.** Besides, Brio came over not too long after that.

"**It's time,**" he said, in an extremely serious tone.

I blinked. "Time for what?"

Then he smiled—**but ever so slightly.**

"Time to make posters,
of course."

OUR WALL
WILL NEVER FALL.

So cute!

Even now it feels **unreal** to me, like this is all just a dream.

Here's another thing I thought I'd **never** actually see.

RUNT
STUDENT
LEVEL 95

MINING	87%
COMBAT	100%
TRADING	100%
FARMING	89%
BUILDING	98%
CRAFTING	97%

BOOM!!!

(Like the noise of a row of creepers thinking they're tough hiding behind slimes then getting ignited by flint and steel.)

239

After yesterday's battle, I've become the **second-highest student.** I passed everyone **but Breeze.** Graduation is right around the corner, too.

All I have to do is hold onto my ranking. Make sure no one **sabotages** me.

Pebble, I'm watching you . . . !!

In less than thirty minutes, Breeze and I finished **our posters.** We rejoined the **celebration** to open arms and cheers. Stump gave me a **high five.** He'd heard from the other teachers about my rank in school. He wasn't doing bad himself—**seventh place.**

I promised to help get him **up there.** How could I not? How could I fight hordes of monsters without my **BFF,** my buddy, my pal? The friend in question retrieved a **strange,** box-like item from his inventory.

"Look what I **crafted**," he said.

I stared at the curious-looking item. I'd **never** seen anything like it before.

"The humans were telling me about how they have these things called **birthday parties,** where they eat **cake** and open **presents.** And this . . . is a **present.**" He shoved the box into my hands.

"Um, **thanks.**" I stared at the colorful item again. "So what am I supposed to do with it, exactly?"

"Well, it's like a gift—"

Gift . . . ?
As in, free cool stuff?

I immediately knew what I was supposed to do with this item.

Literally **0.0000000001** seconds after that word came out of his mouth . . .

I knew what to do.

*No, I'm not eating it—those pieces are flying from my excited little hands. By the way, you can't see my hands because **they're moving that fast.***

241

As **quickly** as I'd opened it, the wrapping faded to reveal . . .
a diamond.

A diamond!!!

I don't need to tell you how **super mega rare** diamonds
are in my village. Even so, I'd like to share a little story to help
you fully understand. There had been **a bunch of diamonds** in
a **storeroom** somewhere, including the ones from that double ore
vein we'd found. The mayor had been saving them for the **right
time.** Before that time had come, though, **Urf** decided to **betray**
us. Now there are **zero diamonds.**

The miners have been digging deeper and deeper in recent days,
trying to find more. So far, **nothing.** Not a single new vein. Actually,
even iron ore is rare now. In the countless layers of stone beneath our
village, we've already mined up almost everything.

Even stone. We extracted a great deal of stone for our constant
building, leaving huge, dark tunnels. Now those mine tunnels extend far
and wide, in confusing twists, like a **giant maze** with many levels.
Endless corridors of stone and gravel entirely picked clean.

242

In short, we're running out of **resources.** We have a continual supply of wood from the tree farm, but you can't grow new ore. For this reason, the miners grew **frantic.** The mayor has been pushing them to find more.

So they started working harder and faster. Deep down, in **Tunnel 67**, one of them opened up a hole into a **dungeon** of some kind. The chamber they broke into was **massive.** Their torchlight barely reached the ceiling. The opposite walls couldn't be seen. Just inky darkness. Whatever that place was, it was huge—and most likely filled with **treasure chests, gold, emeralds, weapons, armor, and the relics of a forgotten time.**

At first, the miners were too excited. After all, there were probably diamonds in there as well. Yet as soon as they entered, they heard this **horrible hissing.** Heard something moving in the darkness beyond their torchlight. Whatever it was, it was big. **Really big.** An enormous spider, perhaps. Or something not found in any of our books on ancient monsters.

243

Well, those miners aren't **noobs.** There's a reason why they're still alive after working down there for so long. They climbed right back out, sealed up that hole, and sealed off the mine tunnel leading to it—with **five layers of cobblestone,** no less.

Later, they put numerous **signs** around the area, warning everyone not to enter. **They even made a fence.**

NOT ALLOWED

DANGER

67

BAD

NO DIAMONDS

LEAVE

RUN

VERY BAD

I just hope humans don't wander by some day. They might whip out their pickaxes thinking they've found our secret stash.

I gazed down at the **diamond** resting gently in my hands. Considering all of that, I had to wonder how many emeralds Stump had to trade for it. My friend just shrugged, like he'd given me a loaf of bread instead of **an amazingly awesome** gemstone.

"I know you've been wanting **a better sword**," he said, "so I thought I'd try to help out. We should find a good crafter."

". . ."

I was so **overwhelmed** that I didn't know **what to say.** Stump seemed to understand what I was thinking, though.

"Don't worry about **repaying** me," he said. "You already have. By being **my best friend.**"

"**Thanks,**" I said. "I want to say—"

I paused mid-sentence. Around me, everyone else had stopped talking. One by one, their heads were slowly turning to—

THE MAYOR.

He was standing on the raised platform again. He had that **gloomy** expression he was famous for, which meant it was time to listen.

245

"I have one more **announcement** today," he said. "I've discussed our mob situation with the rest of the leaders, and . . ."

There was a long silence.

". . . we've decided that any student graduating this year may choose the **Path of the Sword.**"

Path.

That's what many of the older villagers call **professions.** There's the **Path of the Seed, Path of the Fishing Rod, Path of the Book and Quill,** and so on. Every year, the village holds a ceremony in which those graduating must choose one **item** from a special chest. They then hold it proudly above their head, in front of everyone, to show what **Path (and profession) they have chosen.** It's a **permanent** decision. **No looking back.** Like always, that chest will be filled with items like fishing rods, pickaxes, cobblestone, books, anvils, crafting tables, wool, leather . . .

But this year,
it's also going to contain **swords.**

In other words, everyone can become a warrior, regardless of his or her rank. Although I was shocked by this big reveal, in a way, I'd always been expecting it.

With so many mobs running around now, how could five villagers keep things under control? At this point, we need a small army.

Maybe the humans will eventually shape up and all start fighting. Even if they did, it wouldn't be enough, and we couldn't expect them to stick around and protect us forever. No, this was something that had to happen. It was inevitable, really. The only real question is—what about the top five?

Was all of my hard work for nothing? All of my studying and constant risk-taking? A few students voiced the same concern. In response, the mayor nodded in a knowing way, perhaps expecting this reaction.

"Of course, those graduating with the highest rank will not go unrewarded. They'll have the option of choosing a special path.

The Path of the Diamond.

Now beside him, Brio spoke up.

"Diamonds are valued for their purity, rarity, brilliance, and durability . . . just like anyone who follows this Path. You will lead our warriors into battle. **You will devise combat strategies.** You will lead us to victory as **captains. Our fighting elite.**

"And someday," Drill added, "you will lead our warriors to the **very gates of Herobrine's castle itself!**"

The mayor turned to him angrily. **"Fool!"** He glanced down at the **bottle of melon juice** Drill was holding. Then he leaned over to the combat teacher, took a sniff, and **slapped** the bottle out of his hand. **"Fermented!** I should have known!"

"**Fermented?**" Drill glanced at the bottle as it rolled away across the cobblestones. "What are you talking about?"

Fermented melon juice. Sure. That explained a lot. After the girls' discovery of this recipe, they'd found that adding a fermented **spider eye** would change normal melon juice into a fermented variety.

Upon drinking it, a person is affected by a debuff. The debuff makes it **hard to walk** in addition to other weird side effects, like being **extremely forgetful,** having **difficulty concentrating, slurred speech . . .**

So strange. Since this is a newly discovered recipe, and since Drill doesn't know much about **brewing or crafting,** he wouldn't have been able to tell the difference.

248

He could have noticed the distinctive sour smell, sure, but maybe he hadn't been paying attention. Of course, even Drill knew that this was no accident. Someone must have served him that juice on purpose.

"If I ever find out which one of you did this," he roared at the students, "after you're done doing push-ups, you're gonna resemble a creeper!!"

(I'm guessing he meant their arms were going to fall off?)

With how many students were giggling right then, there was no way to tell who the trickster was. But the mischievous grin Max was trying to conceal told me all I needed to know. I doubt he'd expected his prank to cause so much chaos, however. Anyway, it didn't matter. The truth was already out. The mayor sighed and hung his head. Brio ushered the angry combat teacher away, and the students' laughter soon faded.

Then there was only eerie silence. Perhaps all one hundred and fifty students were contemplating what Drill had blurted out.

The gates of Herobrine's castle.

249

The end . . . For now!!

Read the dramatic conclusion in book 4:

Diary of an 8-Bit Warrior:
Path of the Diamond

ABOUT THE AUTHOR

Cube Kid is the pen name of Erik Gunnar Taylor, a writer who has lived in Alaska his whole life. A big fan of video games—especially Minecraft—he discovered early that he also had a passion for writing fan fiction.

Cube Kid's unofficial Minecraft fan fiction series, *Diary of a Wimpy Villager*, came out as e-books in 2015 and immediately met with great success in the Minecraft community. They were published in France by 404 éditions in paperback with illustrations by Saboten and now return in this same format to Cube Kid's native country under the title *Diary of an 8-Bit Warrior*.

When not writing, Cube Kid likes to travel, putter with his car, devour fan fiction, and play his favorite video game.